Praise for Lori Copeland's

stranded in paradise

"Copeland's vivid portrayal of a tropical setting and two compelling characters in search of inner peace will delight the senses, tug at the heart, and lift the spirit. A divine read."

LINDA WINDSOR,
award-winning author of the Moonstruck series

"Well-written, stormy, and intense with life and love."

LYN COTE,
author of *Winter's Secret*

"*Stranded in Paradise* gives a new meaning to the term 'island style' as Tess Nelson experiences everything *but* the tropical bliss she was hoping to find on Maui. Grab your sunglasses and come along for the frolic!"

ROBIN JONES GUNN,
award-winning author of *Gardenias for Breakfast*

"Enchanting! Lori Copeland's lively, riveting writing style and cast of quirky characters engaged me from the moment I started reading. Exciting action sprinkled with Lori's trademark humor held my attention as I drank in the deep spiritual truth of the importance of total surrender to Christ."

CATHERINE PALMER,
Christy Award-winning author of *The Happy Room* and
English Ivy

"This great story is Copeland at her best. I highly recommend it!"

COLLEEN COBLE,
author of *Alaska Twilight*

"I've loved Lori Copeland's writing for years, and her latest effort is no exception. Reminiscent of yesteryear's cinematic romantic comedies, *Stranded in Paradise* employs situational humor that is never slapstick, but is long on fun and love. Lori goes a step further to blend in a gentle, but powerful message of faith."

JANE ORCUTT,
author of *Lullaby* and *The Living Stone*

"Descriptive and compelling. In *Stranded in Paradise*, award-winning Lori Copeland offered me a cozy, satisfying read with a subtle humor that caused a chuckle, a tender love story that brought tears, and a heroine whose flickering faith erupted into a triumphant blaze."

"*Stranded in Paradise* is a beautiful story of love and redemption. Lori Copeland's wonderfully witty tale takes you on the vacation you never wanted and makes you so very glad you went. Romance, the tropics, and a strong inspirational theme make *Stranded in Paradise* a sure winner!"

"I just took a wonderful trip to Hawaii with Lori Copeland and didn't even have to board a jet. From the frozen skies of Denver to the wild tropical breezes of a Maui hurricane, [*Stranded in Paradise* kept] me guessing with little surprises all along the way. I'm looking forward to the next exciting getaway with this gifted writer."

stranded in paradise

The Women of Faith Fiction Club presents

stranded in
paradise

A Story of Letting Go

BY LORI COPELAND

THOMAS NELSON
Since 1798

NASHVILLE DALLAS MEXICO CITY RIO DE JANEIRO BEIJING

Published in Nashville, Tennessee, by Thomas Nelson. Thomas Nelson is a registered trademark of Thomas Nelson, Inc.

Published in association with the literary agency of Alive Communications, Inc., 7680 Goddard Street, Suite 200, Colorado Springs, Colorado, 80920. All rights reserved.

Thomas Nelson books may be purchased in bulk for educational, business, fund-raising, or sales promotional use. For information, please e-mail SpecialMarkets@ThomasNelson.com.

The Holy Bible, New Living Translation (NLT) © 1996. Used by permission of Tyndale House Publishers, Inc., Wheaton, Ill. All rights reserved.

This is a work of fiction. Names, characters, places, and incidents either are the product of the author's imagination or are used fictitiously. Any resemblance to actual persons, living or dead, events, organizations, or locales is entirely coincidental.

Library of Congress Cataloging-in-Publication Data

Copeland, Lori.
     Stranded in paradise / by Lori Copeland.
       p. cm.
     ISBN 978-1-59554-617-3 (repak)
     ISBN 978-1-59554-643-2 (se)
     1. Colorado—Fiction. I. Title.
   PS3553.O6336 S77 2002
   813'.54—dc21
2002008987

Printed in the United States of America

08 09 10 11 12 QW 7 6 5 4 3 2 1

This book is a singular gift from God, and I praise His name that He would allow this author to extol His glory through Women of Faith.

And to Thelma Jean Keithly Bilyeu: mother of nine children, grandmother of twenty-two, great-grandmother of twenty-one, and great-great-grandmother of one. Thelma was called home to be with the Lord as I was finishing this book. A devoted follower of Christ, Thelma enjoyed many hours of Christian fiction. Thelma, you will be sorely missed by family, friends, and loved ones. Until we meet again . . .

*Let the L*ORD*'s people show him reverence, for those who honor him will have all they need. Even strong young lions sometimes go hungry, but those who trust in the L*ORD *will never lack any good thing.*

—PSALM 34:9–10

1

"Boy, Kim, this weather is nutty, isn't it? Where's the *snow*?"

"Rocky, I don't know," the female disk jockey deadpanned. "We don't have to worry about hurricanes here in Denver land: I WANT SNOW!"

Tess Nelson signaled, then switched lanes on the busy interstate. The Acura surged ahead, passing a slower-moving vehicle before shooting back to the right lane. The digital clock turned to 8:56 AM.

The disk jockeys kept up their banter. "Imagine a summer thunderstorm, a dark, hulking brute towering over ten turbulent miles into the heavens—black, rolling clouds spewing blinding rain, hailstones, and lightning. Then picture a line of these monsters seventy-five miles long, standing shoulder to shoulder," Rocky said of an approaching storm in the South Pacific. "Take that line and wrap it around into a circle 230 miles across and spin it counterclockwise at 140 miles an hour and you're in the eye of a hurricane. . . . Must be something to experience . . ." She frowned at the radio, as she wondered how long it took for those storms to fizzle out. She had a business trip planned for the following week in Hawaii, and the last thing she needed was some tropical depression to foul up her plans.

The Acura wheeled into the underground parking garage. Tires and power steering screeched as she ascended from the first floor to the second level. She turned into spot seven, shut off the engine, and looked at the clock. 8:57—oops. 8:58. On time.

Her newest twenty-something temp was waiting when the elevator doors opened to the fourteenth floor.

"Suit wants to see you in his office." Judy chewed gum and pointed an acrylic-nailed, three-ringed finger toward the executive suite one floor up.

"I need to drop these things off in my office and get a cup of coffee—"

"No time, kiddo. The Man says now. Mucho pronto." The temp blew a bubble and popped it back into her mouth in one swift move.

Tess shifted the armload of folders, sunglasses, briefcase, and purse, then pilfered a notepad and pen from her secretary's desk. "Please spit out your gum." She pointed to the wastebasket.

"Yes, ma'am."

Ma'am? Tess flinched. She had to speak to Nick in personnel about the help he was sending her lately. The last one had taken breaks every hour to do her yoga stretches right there on the office floor. She didn't know how long she could deal with the endless array of teenyboppers behind the desk.

Stepping into the elevator, she punched floor thirty-seven and tapped the pen against the notepad as she watched the numbers change above the elevator's doors. To hear Len refer to the executive office as "his office" sounded strange. He'd taken over as chief executive officer of Connor.com upon the sudden death of his father, Dave Connor, the man who had started the company five years earlier. While dot com companies had been rising fast in the late nineties, Dave Connor had moved with caution, investing back into the business instead of buying new equipment and hiring employees he wouldn't be able to keep for the long haul. He was a man of vision. But Dave hadn't planned on dying at the age of sixty-one of a heart attack.

Dot com companies sell service, not a product,

and Dave had built a strong, self-sustaining business because he cared about his customers. Connor.com allowed clients to place bids on large-ticket or small-ticket items online. If they wished, they could even do a closed bid.

Under Dave's management, changes were constantly made to meet a client's needs. Most of the schools in this area used Connor.com to order supplies like hand soap, detergent, grease-breaker soap, and soap for mopping kitchen floors, tile floors, and hardwood floors. One catalog they maintained listed over twenty thousand different soap items.

A company of this size needed a lot of people: a chief executive officer, chief financial officer, chief operations officer, chief technical officer, plus middle management people and a ton of technical geeks. Not everyone could manage a company this size the way Dave had done. She hoped Len was up to it.

Tess had met Dave at a Chamber of Commerce mixer five and a half years ago. He was a kind man who had treated her like a daughter almost from the time they met. When he had asked her to join his company a few months later, she'd jumped at the opportunity.

The job was a human resource manager's dream, with a lot of potential for advancement. She was ready for the challenges. For the past two years Dave had been grooming her to take the position of vice president of human resources, second in command of Connor.com.

Apparently, this morning Len was ready to announce that he was moving her into the job. She knew she was ready to steer the company through the turbulent waters of mergers and acquisitions, setting up profit sharing and a 401(k) program that would attract experienced and loyal employees. This was the crowning achievement of all her hard work.

As she reached Len's office, his secretary, Nancy, was coming out. "Hello," Tess chirped.

"Go on in," Nancy murmured, refusing to meet her eye. Odd. Nancy Silva was one of the friendliest people Tess knew. From the look on Nancy's face she wondered if something awful had happened to her.

"Thanks," Tess said as Nancy turned her back.

She opened the door. Len had made few changes to Dave's office. When she entered the world of mahogany and Prussian blue she found Len leaning back in Dave's chair, phone to his ear, staring out the big window behind the large desk that had been his father's for over twenty years. Len had that familiar pose, forefinger tapping the back of the phone as he spoke, as if prompting whoever was on the other end to hurry it up. His sandy hair fell against his forehead in that boyish way he had. Tess felt her back stiffen as the old feelings tried to wedge their way back in. Yes, Len had his charms, she told herself, but there was a selfish side to the man.

"See you the first of the week," Len said into the receiver, then hung up the phone and swung around. "Ah, Tess."

She smiled, reminding herself of what this meeting was no doubt about. "Ah, Len." She'd waited a long time for this moment, put in many a long day and given up countless weekends to make deadlines.

She sobered when he didn't return her smile, and uneasiness grew in the pit of her stomach. His life had changed tremendously when Dave died, she reasoned, he was just having a hard day.

She could be of invaluable help now that Dave was gone, of course, and she would. She knew the ins and outs of the company better than anyone, Len included. "Have a seat," Len invited.

She sank into one of the familiar leather chairs where she'd spent many an evening after five sitting, talking business, and laughing over Dave's corny jokes. She wondered briefly if she and Len would have the same kind of relaxed, creative relationship after working hours. Maybe the man could change. She looked up into his eyes.

"You know the dot com business is a little bizarre right now, with so many companies folding," Len said quickly as he raked a hand through his blond hair.

"Yes . . ." Tess replied uncertainly, wondering where he was headed. Was Len thinking of merging with another company? Connor.com was financially stable, but right now wasn't the best time—

"The good news is a lot of qualified people are suddenly available."

She shrugged. "True."

"I was talking to a friend I went to college with. We were fraternity brothers, in fact."

"Oh?" She crossed her legs and focused on him, wishing he'd get to the point. "What's his background?"

"Chuck Vinton has been V.P. of human resources at a West Coast firm, but they were bought out . . ."

A prickle of apprehension snaked down her spine.

"—and he's free, so I've hired him as our new vice president."

For a split second, she felt nothing, as if she were in a tunnel without sound or reason. Vice president, he had said—vice president of human resources.

"I don't understand," she said through her fog.

Len met her eyes. He enunciated the words this time, speaking slowly as if she were unable to comprehend. "Chuck's going to take over. He's exactly what Connor.com needs."

Tess shifted forward in her chair. "You hired a *fraternity* brother for my job?"

"I knew you would have a hard time with this, Tess. Chuck isn't exactly taking your position. Your situation here with Connor.com has been unusual—Dad gave you a lot of responsibility. He may have made promises but that was when he was . . ."

"Promises be hanged! Len, you know me. I've worked seventy-hour weeks, skipped vacations, erased my personal life—"

"And I appreciate your hard work, but I think the company's better served by hiring someone with more experience. Chuck has ten years under his belt."

He toyed with an eraser, sitting up in his chair to slam dunk the rubber into a glass ashtray.

She seethed. Her life was falling apart, and the dunce was shooting hoops.

So there it was: all her hard work, setting up the department from the company's foundation, was being tossed aside because Len Connor ran into an old college buddy. She should have known he'd pull something like this.

"I see." She struggled to hold on to some shred of professionalism. "Then you're saying that I will be working for Mr. Vinton."

Len swirled a gold pen between his fingers. "Well, you *could,* I guess, but the thing is . . ." He paused, and she could see his jaw tense. "Chuck is bringing his own people; you'll have to apply for any openings that are left."

"He's bringing—" She tried to absorb the shock. Her mind whirled. "So either I start from square one or I'm fired?"

Len shrugged. "Sorry."

"You're *firing* me?" She stood up, pen and pad fluttering to the floor. The Uniball rolled under the desk.

"There is another open position in which you would fit well—"

"Where?" Her voice was almost a screech.

"Payroll." He smiled, but there was a hint of condescension in that twinkle in his eyes.

Her lashes narrowed. "You're offering me a job in *payroll?*"

He lifted his shoulders. "It's a good position. Decent pay. Punch out at five o'clock."

She stopped him cold. "I am a manager, Len, not a payroll clerk. I have five years of experience hiring and managing *departments* full of payroll clerks and a dozen other employees. Len, this is a huge professional insult!"

His tone firmed. "I'm only doing what's best for Connor.com. You know that we've tightened our belts, that we've frozen new hires—"

Anger welled inside her.

"But you can bring in your fraternity brother and *his* people? Do I look that stupid, Len?"

He shifted closer to the desk. Beneath the polished wood, his foot tapped erratically. "Your years of service have been duly noted, Tess. It's a tough break, but you're resilient. In a few years, who knows, maybe you'll prove me wrong."

She swallowed back an acid retort. "I'm thinking you're right. I can do better than Conner.com. Chuck does sound like the man to head the helm."

Len shrugged. "Of course the choice is yours. Perhaps you need a few days to think about it . . ."

"I don't need a *vacation*." Right now she needed a two-by-four. A good solid plank to wipe the smirk off his silver-spoon-fed Harvard face.

He calmly met her wintry stare. "I'll hold the payroll position until I hear from you." The phone rang and he picked it up, dismissing her with a nod.

She pivoted on her heels and walked out.

Fired.

Sacked.

She had just been squeezed out—regardless of the "options" Len thought he was giving her. Payroll indeed!

Vaguely aware that Len's secretary was bent conspicuously over a file cabinet, she mustered a pleasant smile and made her way out.

Ducking into the executive washroom, Tess locked herself in a stall, refusing to cry—crying would leave her eyes red and puffy—but she breathed deeply for several minutes as she tried to harness her emotions. She would keep her dignity if it killed her.

Minutes later, she wet a paper towel and pressed it to her eyes, checked to ensure that her makeup was still flawless, then she returned to her office. There, laying on the top of her desk, sat the airline ticket for her business trip. A lot of good that was. The airline wouldn't allow her to transfer it into another name.

She stood staring at it. It would serve Len right to lose the cost of the ticket. She wondered why he hadn't mentioned her upcoming trip. Maybe he'd forgotten. She lifted the envelope and turned it over in her hands. Then in one swift move she tucked it into her briefcase. She wasn't sure why.

She had to get out of the office before she started blubbering, or worse yet before she went back and gave Len Connor a piece of her mind. She reached for her purse and briefcase, then, lifting her chin, walked quickly to the elevator. Len Connor would soon discover that Tess Nelson couldn't be replaced by a fraternity brother or anyone else.

The perky temp went on point. "Are you leaving for the day, Miss Nelson?"

"I'll be out of the office a couple of weeks," she said weakly. Maybe by then Len will have called begging her to come back. She pushed the lighted button, aware of the curious eyes following her. She straightened, her chin lifting a notch. She knew that news of her firing would spread faster than small-town gossip once she left the building. Would anyone care that she'd been dumped? She doubted it; she'd made few friends among her coworkers, but who had time for a social life with her workload? Anyway, she wasn't there to socialize. She was there to work. As they should be. That was how she'd gotten where she was, after all . . .

Mona.

The dread word surfaced in her consciousness as she rode to the ground floor. She could hear her mother's voice now: *Well, the news doesn't surprise me. You always mess up somehow.* She slid into her Acura and flipped on the car defrosters. As she drove out of the garage, she realized that the rain was falling in sheets. She pulled into traffic, erratically swerving to miss an oncoming public transportation bus.

Len Connor could not humiliate her this way. She had helped his father build Connor.com. She couldn't be replaced by a ruthless whim, and that was all this ploy was. Len had always been jealous of the trust his father had put in her. Now that he was in charge he was rubbing her nose in it.

But he'd see Connor.com couldn't run without her—and it wouldn't take Len long to recognize it. Not once things started falling apart.

Tess unlocked the door to her condo and flicked on the light. More than anything else, her home was a deliberate reminder of how far up the ladder she had climbed. Colonial blue walls with white trim, white sofa, blue-and-white striped Queen Anne chairs, a tall lemon-yellow vase holding a silk arrangement of willows and forsythia had all been chosen to create an impression of pristine cleanliness. She remembered the dirty, dismal house she had grown up in and shuddered. How had she survived?

Shucking off her shoes, she made her way to the kitchen, where she scooped up a bowl of ice cream and topped it with a drizzle of Hershey's syrup. She dug her spoon in and lifted it to her mouth when she noticed a long hair trailing out of it. "Eww!" She groaned and gazed down at the counter where three more strands innocently lay. "Not again," she said.

She set the ice cream down and made her way to the bathroom where she studied herself in the mirror. It didn't *look* like she was losing her hair, but lately it seemed as if she'd found strands everywhere: in her checkbook, on reports for work, in her food . . .

She lifted a brush from the counter and gave her taffy-color hair a few strokes when the phone began jangling.

"Tess?" a voice said when she picked up.

"Beeg?" Tess said. Bee Gee had been her college roommate. She'd since made a name for herself as an artist working primarily in watercolor.

"Say, I was calling about your trip next week. There's this show in New York—"

"Oh, Beeg!" she moaned, the tears she'd so carefully held in now flowing freely. "That—that oaf Len Connor had the gall to fire me this morning! Can you believe this?"

"Oh, honey," Beeg consoled. "I'm so sorry."

Tess sobbed in big gulps. "He actually thought I'd take a job in *payroll* when he knows I've been practically running the company these past few months."

"So, what are you going to do about it? How high up is his office? Maybe you could throw rocks at his window."

That brought a smile to Tess's waterlogged cheeks.

"You always could cheer me up."

"Maybe you should come next week anyway. It could be a vacation instead of a business trip. I'm sure you have money squirreled away."

"I do still have the ticket . . ." She glanced at her briefcase by the door. "But it wouldn't be right. I didn't pay for it."

"Was it right for Len Connor to fire you?" Beeg defended.

"No . . ."

"So you need time to regroup, think through what you want to do next. What better place than in Hawaii with your best friend?"

"You know I'd love to spend some time with you," Tess began, "but I just don't know if I'm ready now. There's just too much . . ."

"And your perfect little schedule can't adjust?" Beeg said with kindness in her voice. "I know all about it. But if you change your mind . . ."

"I know where to find you," she finished, and Beeg chuckled.

"In the meantime," Beeg said, "why don't you go find some nice big rocks to throw at that window? Boulders, maybe."

After she hung up the phone, Tess returned to her ice cream and sat at the kitchen table as she ate. It had been at least six years since she'd seen Bee Gee

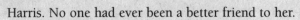

Harris. No one had ever been a better friend to her.

She held her spoon up, gazing at her reflection in the concave surface that made her nose look disproportionately large. She laughed aloud, then realized how hollow it sounded in the silence of her home.

Maybe it would be good to go see Beeg, she thought. At least she'd have someone to have a good cry with. Who knew, maybe some time on a Hawaiian beach would give her the direction she needed.

Jan. 14, 2:30 PM
O'Hare International Control Tower

Carter McConnell sat at his terminal and watched snow blowing in driving sheets against the tower windows. Perched in the glassed-in birdcage, weary air traffic controllers gazed at their radar monitors.

It had been one of the worst nights anyone could remember. During the past few hours they had efficiently handled close to four hundred incoming and outgoing flights. Planes were sitting at gates, others systematically landing and taking off, but the rush was nothing compared to what it had been earlier.

From his vantage point high atop the airport terminal, Carter focused on the red beacon lights moving about the runway. He wished he were home. His head ached and his throat felt scratchy and tight. He wanted to kick back, relax, give his dog, Max, a tummy rub, and eat a nice bowl of mint chocolate chip ice cream. But he still had an hour before his shift was over.

He glanced at the ground-surveillance radar and suddenly sat up straighter. A quick reading on the bright display indicated that a United Boeing 727, still ten miles out, was coming in fast. Carter quickly flipped a switch on the panel in front of him.

"Approach, this is Ground. Clipper 242 looks to be coming in hard. Does he have a problem?"

"Ground, this is Approach. Yeah, he's picking up heavy ice. He's been cleared to land on Runway 36."

Carter glanced at the ground radar again and frowned. If Tim Matthews, the approach controller, had accurate information, they were in trouble. Carter's ground-surveillance screen indicated an unidentified airplane taxiing toward the approach end of Runway 36.

Carter grabbed the binoculars and scanned the snow-covered tarmac. His jaw clenched when he saw the lighted tail section of a Global Airways DC-9 disappearing toward the runway.

"Global, this is Ground—" The sharp crackling at the other end took Carter by surprise. "Global, this is Ground. Do you read me?" The question was met with an ominous silence. Flipping a second switch, Carter shouted, "Local, we've got a problem. I've got a Global Airways DC-9 taxiing on Runway 36 and a Boeing 727 about to land on him. He's not responding!" His voice rose another decibel.

"What's he doing out there?" a voice screeched over the airwaves.

"That's what I'm trying to find out. Advise the Clipper."

"Roger." Max Lakin flipped a switch on his panel. "Clipper 242 be advised we have a no-radio Global DC-9 taxiing southbound on Runway 36. Be prepared for a go-around."

The Clipper's pilot came back. "Local, what's the Global doing out there?"

"Beats me. We're trying to reach the aircraft."

"I'm low on fuel. You're gonna have to get him out of there!" the United pilot shot back.

Carter listened as he kept a close eye on the runway visual-radar indicator. Visibility was down to 2,400 feet. For the past four and a half hours the pilots had been relying solely on instruments.

The nerves between his shoulder blades tightened as he hit the radio switch again.

"Global DC-9, this is Ground." Carter's urgency seeped through his voice. "Exit runway immediately! Do you hear me?"

Wiping a shaky hand across the back of his neck, he eased forward in his chair as the tower supervisor threw down the papers he had been reading and came to stand behind him.

"What's going on?"

"I've got an unauthorized DC-9 taxiing on a reserved runway and he's not talking to me."

Carl Anderson frowned. He was fiftyish, with a large waist and graying hair.

"He obviously thinks he's been cleared," Carter muttered. He tried to reach the DC-9 again. "Global DC-9, exit to taxiway immediately! Repeat. Exit to taxiway immediately!"

Carl leaned over Carter's shoulder and watched the screen as the two planes continued on their courses on Runway 36.

"Tell Local to advise Clipper to go around," Carl said as Carter started pressing the necessary switches.

"I'll try it again—Local, this is Ground. Advise Clipper 242. Unauthorized DC-9 still on runway. Go around immediately! Repeat. Go around immediately!"

"Roger!" Local quickly punched another switch. "Clipper 242, this is Local. Aircraft on runway. Go around. Repeat. Go around."

Carter heard Local talking to the Clipper. Then he heard the pilot's voice, "I'd love to oblige, Local, but this ain't no crop duster I'm flyin'."

"Well, you'd better find a way, Clipper, unless you want to be headline news tomorrow morning," Carter warned. He watched the screen as the two dots drew closer.

All Carter could hope for was that the timing of the two aircraft would be a split second apart and a collision would be avoided. He breathed a silent prayer: *Lord, I've done all I can do on this end. It's up to You.*

Carl hurriedly reached for the crash phone to alert the fire station and emergency crew of an impending crisis. Carter tried to raise the Global DC-9 again, "Global, exit to taxiway *immediately!* Repeat. Exit to taxiway *immediately!*"

Riveted to the screen, the men watched in tense silence as the two blips on the radar screen rushed closer and closer together. The room had become unnaturally quiet as the other flight controllers performed their duties in hushed tones.

"Well, start praying," Carl advised.

"Already have."

The wide-bodied Boeing 747 touched down on the landing strip and came streaking along the runway as the DC-9 inched its way forward.

"Move it, move it, move it," Carter breathed, then he held his breath as the plane rolled laboriously across the path of the incoming 747.

The strained voice of the Clipper pilot cracked over the wire, "Get out of the way, buddy!" Carter cringed as the pilot's voice willed the DC-9 out of his path.

The dots closed in on each other on Carter's screen as the Clipper roared down the landing strip at more than two hundred miles per hour. The blips grew closer and closer.

Suddenly they split apart, and the DC-9 eased off the runway as the 747 shot by him in a screech of flying mud and snow.

Carter threw down his pencil and leaned back in his chair weakly as Carl let out a loud war whoop.

"Thank you, God!" Carter said.

"What was that?" yelled the pilot of the DC-9 over the wire, the man obviously shaken.

"Global, you're on an unauthorized taxiway!" Carter snapped. "Where have you been? I've been trying to contact you for three minutes."

"I'm sorry. We've had a radio malfunction—I just heard the contact . . ."

"Well, take some advice, when you have a radio problem don't just go strolling down a runway!" Carter flipped off the radio switch and rubbed his face with his hands. He was trembling and flushed.

Carl laid his hands on his shoulders and gave them a supportive squeeze. "You okay?"

Emotionally and physically drained, Carter could not will himself to respond. He leaned back in his chair and stared at the ceiling. There was no longer any doubt about it. The pressure of the job was getting to him. True, he'd experienced closer calls, but his palms had never felt so sweaty or his stomach been in such a tight knot.

When Carl had hired him nine years earlier, Carter had been self-confident; he'd have brushed off this sort of incident without another thought, considering it a part of the business. Perhaps be energized by it, even. But tonight was different. It shouldn't be. He was a seasoned professional, but tonight was— enough. It was enough. He couldn't do this any more.

His supervisor clapped a friendly hand on his shoulder. "Come to my office when you get a minute."

Carter's pulse jumped. "Sure."

His supervisor was on the phone when he arrived. He glanced up and motioned Carter to help himself to the coffee. Carter shook his head. The last thing he needed was more caffeine in his system. He settled his large frame into the upholstered chair opposite Carl's desk.

Carl finished his conversation in a few moments.

"Sorry." He nodded toward the phone. "The higher-ups drive me crazy."

"No problem."

The older man stepped to the hotplate and picked up a carafe. "One more cup of this stuff is gonna kill me. Wanda would have a fit if she knew how many I've had today." He shrugged, then poured the strong black brew into his cup and added a couple packets of sugar. "I'm going to die of something, so I figure I might as well go alert."

Carter acknowledged Carl's attempt at wit with a slim smile and waited patiently until he sat down again. Carl was always worrying about what his wife thought about his bad habits, but never enough to change them.

Carl sipped the strong coffee cautiously, then sipped again. He seemed to be doing a lot of fidgeting. Carter wished he'd get to the point of the pow-wow. "You're doing a great job, son," Carl finally said, meeting Carter's eyes. He set his foam cup aside and leaned forward on his forearms.

Carter glanced up, surprised by the unexpected praise. "Thanks."

"I'm sending you on a vacation."

The statement was firm and straight to the point.

"Vacation? I can't. Not right now."

"Sure you can. You leave tomorrow morning."

"Come on, Carl—"

He was about to argue the point when he saw determination creep into his supervisor's face. He could sit here and argue all day, but in the end Carl would have the last word. He always did.

"No buts, buddy." His superior's tone may have softened, but Carter knew his resolution hadn't. "In the past nine years how many vacations have you taken?" He looked Carter in the eye.

"Well . . . I . . ." Carter stammered.

"You're too valuable a controller for me to lose. I've sat by and watched you for weeks now, and I think it's time we did something. We all reach the end of our limit at some point—most boys take a lot less than nine years to get there. You deserve some time away."

Carter knew better than to disagree. He hadn't been himself lately.

"Sorry, Carl, I know I haven't been giving you my best."

Carl leaned back in his chair and studied his coffee cup. "You're one of the most conscientious, moral men I have. I'm only trying to see that I don't lose you. You're tired, Carter. I hate to call it burnout, but something's affecting you both physically and mentally. You need a little R and R. Relax. Have some fun. Forget about the job and its pressures."

"You're worried about my competency."

"You're top-notch, Carter, but this is a high-stress job. We all need a little down time." Carl leaned forward, and his eyes held Carter's gaze. "Look, it's nothing to be ashamed of. We all have our limits. You're conscientious, focused. That's good. But this sort of concentration takes a lot out of a man. A couple weeks of lying in the sun and you'll be back complaining that you've used up all your vacation hours. As far back as I can remember you've used your vacation time for church mission trips to Uganda to help build houses for orphan children. That's good, and God bless you, son, but you need to take time for yourself. Even Christ took time to renew Himself with His Father. You should do the same. Besides, you can fly anywhere in the world for next to nothing. You should take advantage of that."

"My absence will leave you short-handed," Carter reminded. "If I could get over this cold—"

"You will. Bake it out in the sun." Carl grinned.

Carter stood up. While he didn't like being forced to go on vacation, something inside him said he needed it. Two weeks without coping, without thinking, without breaking into a cold sweat, without sitting on the edge of his chair. . . . Maybe rest was all he needed.

"I don't suppose it will do any good to argue with you?"

"None at all. Soon as Randy gets here, consider yourself out of work for the next two weeks, or longer, if you need it. You let me worry about your replacement. That's what I'm paid the big bucks for." He grinned.

Carter reached to shake his supervisor's hand, gratified by the other man's concern. "I appreciate this—"

"Don't worry about it." Carl glanced at his watch. "Uh oh, look at the time. I've got to call Wanda and tell her I'm going to be a few minutes late." He flashed Carter an apologetic grin. "The woman thinks I've dropped dead if I'm not home by six on the dot."

Carter left the tower, groaning when he saw the inch of ice accumulated on his windshield. Starting the motor, he flipped on the defroster and pulled on his gloves as he sat waiting for the windshield to clear.

He knew Carl was right. He'd been working so hard for so long he wasn't even sure he knew *how* to unwind. But the truth was, rest was exactly what he needed. He'd been on "automatic" for too long. And it wasn't an emotional recharging he'd been lacking. He'd transferred his work habits to his spiritual life. He'd been going full-tilt doing "the right things" but not taking time to just be with God—this was the wake-up call he needed and he knew it. Now he only had to think of where he would go to find the sun and privacy he wanted. *Hawaii*—the thought came to him. He'd never seen the island and now was the perfect time. What he needed was a good book, a couple packages of Oreo cookies—chocolate crème peanut butter—and complete solitude for the next two weeks. He could pack everything he needed into a couple of bags. Sun, sand, a hotel with room service, and he was set to go—to regenerate.

2

A yellow cab slowly inched its way along snow-packed Pena Boulevard Tuesday morning. Rain had turned to snow, and the worsening weather was brutal. Traffic to Denver International snarled onto the exit road.

"Will I be able to make my seven o'clock flight?" Tess asked anxiously as she stared out the back window, her warm breath frosty in the cab's arctic air.

"I'll have you there in twenty minutes." The driver peered over his shoulder. "Sorry, the heater's on the fritz. It was working fine an hour ago. Can't imagine what could've happened to it."

She sighed. She'd been in the backseat for the last forty-five minutes of that hour. Why shouldn't the heater fall apart?

The taxi driver peered at her through the rearview mirror.

"Um . . . miss? Are you all right back th—"

KAABOOMMM!

Tess's heart shot to her throat as she instinctively ducked at the sound of the sudden explosion. Briefcase and purse toppled to the floor.

"Ho, boy!" The driver fought the steering wheel and finally managed to ease the cab over to the side of the exit road. "I think we've got ourselves a flat tire."

After bringing the crippled taxi to a halt, he turned halfway around in the driver's seat. "Now, don't worry. I'll get you to your flight on time."

She wanted to *scream*.

As soon as she'd gotten home last night the white stuff had started to fall. Every snowplow in Denver had been working nonstop for the past ten hours. Travel had slowed to a crawl. Six-foot-high drifts made finding a clear spot to pull off the road impossible, but the cab driver managed to get the vehicle off the main thoroughfare. Now an endless string of frustrated motorists inched past the disabled cab, often leaning on their horns as if that would somehow even the score.

"I'll have the tire changed in a jiffy," the driver promised as he got out.

She inched lower in the backseat. What difference did it make? She was going to miss the plane anyway. She would be stuck at the terminal for hours. Why did Len have to do this to her? She ran her hands through her hair, and a clump of strands clung to her hands. *Great,* she thought, *what else could happen?*

No, she wasn't going there; she was going to Hawaii for a nice vacation with her best friend. She would not give Len Connor the satisfaction of ruining her good time.

She was going to relax, consider her options, her career. And she was going to think about it in a lounge chair with a cool fruit drink in her hand in the land of pineapples and grass skirts.

While the driver changed the tire, Tess sat in the frosty silence of the cab, watching snow drift past the car window. The swirling flakes were hypnotic, and she let her mind float back to Len's office and that awful afternoon six days ago. What had happened? She had been so certain that she finally had life under control—

She rested her forehead against the cold windowpane and she laughed humorlessly. *Well, Bee Gee, you don't know what you've gotten yourself into, inviting this nutcase to your house.*

She'd tried to call Beeg a couple of times again last night to confirm their plans, but she'd gotten a busy signal. She'd try again the moment she landed. She should have tried to reach her this morning, but because of the three-hour time difference she'd decided to wait. Besides, Beeg had told her to come.

Her thoughts were interrupted when the cab driver climbed back into the cab. Snow crusted thick on his heavy coat and eyelashes.

"All fixed," he said.

Tess nodded. She had a little over forty minutes to check in and make the gate.

With her luck she would set off the metal detectors, be searched and questioned. She'd miss the flight and have an eight-hour wait before the next one.

"Can you step on it?" she asked. "I'm never going to make my flight."

"Even if I have to make this taxi sprout wings, I'll get you there!" the cabby promised. "I've never caused a passenger to miss a flight yet."

Yes, but you've never had me in your cab. True to his word, the cab driver delivered her in front of United Airlines with thirty minutes to spare. She tore through the crowded terminal, dodging the throng of travelers. The check-in line moved swiftly; she got her boarding pass and made it past security. She had ten minutes left before takeoff time.

As she breathlessly neared the gate, a slow-moving elderly gentleman ahead of her dropped his boarding pass and stooped to retrieve it.

Bags flying, Tess skidded to a stop, gasping in pain when she felt her right ankle give—the same ankle she'd broken in a skiing accident three years before. Fighting the hot sting of wrenched muscles, she bent and collected her briefcase and purse.

The elderly man turned around, apparently oblivious that he had been the cause of her injury. "You okay, little lady? Looks like you had a little tangle."

"Fine." She gritted her teeth against the white-hot pain. "Just dandy."

She straightened. Her ankle throbbed.

"Shouldn't be in such a big hurry. Folks got to learn to slow down. Everyone's in such an all-fired hurry," the man complained as he proceeded slowly on down the corridor, his words of wisdom trailing behind him.

"And 'have a good day' to you, too," she muttered.

She deftly tested her weight on the injured ankle. The ache was awful. She would have to swallow the anguish and hobble on if she was going to make the flight.

She managed to board seconds before the Jetway detached from the plane. Sinking gratefully into her assigned seat, she reached for the seatbelt and fought against the unfamiliar urge to cry. Tess Nelson did not cry. If Mona had taught her one thing it was that a Nelson was in charge of her own life—she and she alone was responsible for herself and her actions. Only whiners and losers cried.

As the 767 roared down the tarmac, she reached to rub her swollen ankle. The pain had turned to a constant ache. She wondered if she would be able to get her boot back on if she took it off during the flight. Deciding some relief from the pressure was worth the risk, she warily pulled off the footwear and examined her ankle. It was puffy, but maybe with luck it wouldn't get any worse. Suddenly aware of the guy setting next to her, she lifted her gaze and met a pair of amused artic blue eyes. A grin hovered at the corners of his tanned features as his gaze dropped to her Nerf-ball-size foot—certainly not her best feature.

Snapping around in her seat, she clicked the belt in place and pretended interest in the in-flight phone. If he said *one* word she would strangle him.

Dropping her head against the headrest, she closed her eyes and felt the familiar tug in her stomach as the plane lifted off and soared into the void of swirling snow. Right now all she wanted to see was a hole open up and swallow the passengers.

"Predicted to add up to fourteen inches before it's over," the radio announcer said. "But we're the lucky ones. Over there in the Pacific, trouble is brewing. A tropical depression has developed. . . . Sustained winds from twenty to thirty-four knots, that's twenty-three to thirty-nine miles per hour, for us lay people. It could turn into a doozy before all's said and done. Stay tuned for further updates."

She tuned out the radio and the teenage boy who wore it. His head bobbed in time with some sort of rap music that she wished was anything else. Even country would've been better. As she returned her tray to the upright position, the "fasten seat belt" sign came on and she settled back to await final descent into Kahului Airport.

At precisely 3:37 PM, Maui time, the Boeing 767 landed. Heavy trade winds gusted through the open walkways as Tess followed the throng of wary fliers

35

to the baggage claim terminal. By now her ankle had swollen to nearly twice its normal size. She had pulled and strained to force her boot back on, groaning aloud in agony. The hunk beside her had looked more than a little awkward at her state, and yet what could he have done? Pushed her bulging ankle from the other side?

Her ankle ached as if a bull had kicked it. She couldn't zip the boot, so the top flapped open, snagging her hose. Her eyes searched the concourse for signs that she was actually in Hawaii. No one met her with a flowered lei, and she didn't spot a single hula girl. Swallowing an odd sense of disappointment, she limped on. Maybe Don Ho was waiting for her in the baggage claim.

I'm in paradise, she thought. *I'm going to relax, bake on the beach, and forget about Len Connor.* She wondered if he'd figured out the new 401(k) deductions they'd worked on with the new investment broker. No doubt *Chuck* would have it all buttoned down in no time.

As she approached baggage claim, an energetic preschooler throwing a full-blown temper tantrum caught her attention. He was screaming and kicking his feet on the floor as his nervous-looking mother pled in a mousy voice, "Now, Tommy, you won't get any gum that way. Please be a good boy for Mommy."

Tommy bounced back up and bolted away from his mother . . . straight at Tess.

Suddenly paralyzed in the face of the oncoming disaster, she tried to sidestep the human missile, but Tommy must've had a homing device because he changed course with her.

The sudden impact knocked her breathless as she threw her weight solidly on her sprained ankle. She bellowed at the sheer agony that shot up her leg as her purse and briefcase went flying. Again.

At precisely the same moment, her right eye blurred. She slapped a hand over her eye to save the dislodged contact, but it was too late.

"Thomas Lee! You stop this moment!" The child's mother marched over to take the little imp by the scruff of the neck from where he lay sprawled at her feet. Tommy's mother turned the child toward her. "What have I told you about running?! Say you're sorry to this nice lady for bumping into her!"

The harried mother turned to Tess, who by now had dropped to her hands and knees and was crawling frantically around on the floor of the terminal, desperately groping for the missing contact lens.

"It's all right," Tess muttered. "I'm sure Thomas didn't mean any harm—" Where was the thing? It couldn't have gone far!

She was as blind as Mr. Magoo without her contacts. She smiled gratefully when other blurs she assumed were people paused to offer help with the search. Soon four other travelers were on their hands and knees scanning the multicolored tile.

The contrite mother had a firm grip on her young son now. The boy stood rooted to the spot as Tess crawled around on the polished floor.

"I'm so sorry about your contact," the mother repeated.

"Don't worry," Tess assured her. "I have my glasses with me."

The boy crossed his arms and looked up at his mother. "Sowwy," he finally managed.

She smiled at the blurred image. "It's quite all right—but don't run anymore. You'll hurt yourself."

The mother ushered her son through the crowd as she gathered her personal belongings and thanked her co-searchers before limping steadfastly toward the luggage carousel.

The luggage hadn't arrived, so she stepped to a nearby pay phone. Her cell phone was buried in her luggage, a mistake she realized in the cab. She searched her purse and coat pockets for change, but all she managed to come up with were six pennies, a nasty-looking nickel that had part of a breath mint stuck to it, and a Canadian coin she had picked up somewhere.

By the time she'd limped to the nearest newsstand for change and limped back, all the phones were in use. She patiently waited while a frazzled-looking housewife gave instructions to her husband and children. "I left some TV dinners in the freezer for tonight. And there's some lettuce and tomatoes for a salad—oh, I forgot to buy Ranch dressing . . ." the woman kept going. When the lady finally ran out of time and dashed off to catch her shuttle ride, Tess moved up to the phone. She dropped her coins into the slot and tapped out Beeg's work number. She breathed a sigh of relief when she heard the phone start to ring—several times with no answer. Replacing the receiver, she frowned. Maybe this was some sort of Hawaiian holiday. She dropped more coins into the phone and dialed Beeg's home number.

Beeg's familiar voice came over the line on the second ring. "Hello! This is Me!"

Relief flooded Tess. Thank goodness. "Hi, Beeg! This is—"

"I'm sorry I can't come to the phone right now,"

her friend's sunny voice interrupted. "At the sound of the tone, please leave your name and number, and I'll return your call as soon as possible."

When she heard the beep, she squeezed her eyes shut in disgust and pressed the receiver against her forehead. *One more delay, Tess. You should be used to that by now.*

Since the luggage was late in arriving, Carter decided to mosey back to the shop. He bought a pineapple-guava-orange smoothie and a copy of *Newsweek,* then walked back to the luggage area. People occupied the benches, so he took a stand near the phones. When he heard the young woman beside him suddenly slam down the receiver, he turned to look.

She fumbled in her coat pocket and extracted a number of tissue wads, which she discarded into the trash receptacle. Finally, she took one wad and held it to her nose as she leaned against the wall and took deep, hiccupping breaths.

He fished a fresh package of tissues from his carry-on and handed it to her, tapping it against her arm to get her attention.

"Thanks," she mumbled, her eyes momentarily meeting his. She wiped her eyes and blew her nose. She looked as if someone had just shot her dog.

"Looks like you're having a rough day," Carter said.

"I've had better," the woman replied, sniffling.

"It could get worse . . ." Carter said. "They could always lose our luggage." He offered her a smile, which she returned shyly.

The woman handed the pack of tissues back.

"Keep it," he said. "I've got more."

"I'm going to sit." She motioned toward her foot. "I . . . hurt my ankle."

He watched as she hobbled over to the waiting area and sat down.

Her shoulders lifted in a sigh as she unwrapped a piece of gum and stuck the stick in her mouth, then blindly fished about with her right hand in her purse, finally withdrawing an emery board. Crossing then uncrossing her legs, she filed her nails and jiggled her left foot erratically.

Busy, busy, busy, Carter thought. He looked around the waiting area. Fifty out of a hundred passengers either had a cell phone pressed to their ear, answered a pager, typed on a laptop, or consulted a hand-held Palm Pal. Looking at them, he realized that he was no different. Until two days ago, he'd been in the same boat, but not anymore. He strengthened his resolve to learn how to be a calm, relaxed person. He didn't want to end up so worn out he was sobbing in front of strangers at the airport.

Ten minutes later, a siren blasted and bags started to drop and roll along the conveyor belt. Easing her way through the throng, Tess eventually found herself standing beside the man who had given her the tissues.

He smiled. "Hello again."

"Hi." They stood, watching. Waiting for their bags. Two hundred and fifty suitcases passed in front of them before she discovered she and the tissue man were the only ones left standing.

He glanced over with a questioning expression in his eyes.

She looked back, shrugging.

She glanced at the baggage opening and prayed that she wouldn't hear the conveyer shut off. The motor continued to hum.

They silently focused on the rotating carousel. Suddenly a single bag belched out of the rubber flaps and lumbered down the belt.

"Finally," she said. "I thought I'd have to go naked *and* blind."

The man ventured a polite, "Huh?"

"I lost my contact earlier."

He grimaced. "I *thought* you looked familiar—you were the woman crawling on the floor."

"Yes, why?" She turned to look at him. "I lost my contact."

He drew a deep breath. "Well, I think I may have stepped on it."

Nostrils flared. Suddenly the air left Kahului terminal. "You did what?"

"I was coming down the corridor and . . . I stepped on what I thought was a piece of hard candy. I'm sorry—"

She shook her head. The information didn't surprise her. "It isn't your fault," she said. "I told you this hasn't been my day. It isn't your fault," she repeated, more to convince herself than him. "I tried to find it, but—"

"Too many big feet." He had a kind smile and eyes that crinkled in the corners.

"You couldn't have known," she said as she latched on to the bag, but his hand grabbed it at the same time.

"Excuse me," he said.

She closed her eyes. "*What* now?"

"I think you're mistaken. This is my bag—see. Big

scar on the right side." He laid his hand across the deep dent in the side of the leather bag.

She evaluated the bag with thinned lips. "No. You're mistaken. This is my bag. Mine has a nick on the left side—received last summer, in New York."

He focused on the piece of black Samsonite. "No, it's mine." He picked up the bag and turned to walk away. Tess felt her temper rising.

She whirled and limped after him. "Wait just one minute! Set my luggage down this very minute!"

He turned around slowly, a look of condescension growing in his eyes.

Dropping the bag on the floor, he then knelt on one knee. "This matter is easily settled. All we have to do is read the nametag. I'm sure you're mistaken."

She stood, heat rising to her cheeks. Their dispute was being closely observed by incoming travelers from other flights, impatient to retrieve their luggage.

"No," she said. "You're mistaken."

Carter pulled the tag free and squinted to read. "Let's see what we have here." Glancing up a moment later, he said solemnly, "I was wrong. The bag isn't mine."

"I know." She smiled. "That's what I've been try-ing to tell you."

He picked up the suitcase and held it out to her. "Here you go, Harry."

Her hand was already wrapping around the handle when the name suddenly penetrated. "Harry?"

He lifted an eyebrow. "You aren't Harry Finnerman?"

"Of course I'm not Harry Finnerman."

"Oh. That's too bad," he said, "because this bag belongs to Harry Finnerman." A grin grew on his face.

"Are you sure?" She squatted to peer at the tag, squinting one eye closed. When she indeed discovered that he was right, she lifted her gaze.

"Don't gloat," she grumbled. "People are watching us." Straightening, she muttered, "Well, I guess my bags are still somewhere."

"As are mine," he agreed.

Just not where any of them are supposed to be.

"I thought you said it couldn't get any worse," she said. He shrugged.

They stepped back to the revolving carousel to wait. A moment later another bag shot out and thundered down the conveyor. Score one more for Harry Finnerman.

A moment later the carousel stopped.

Then a siren blasted, and the conveyor on the right began spitting bags out from a later flight.

"There must have been a mix-up somewhere," the man said quietly.

"Both of my bags are missing," Tess said, feeling her forehead to see if she was getting a fever. No, she was cool. Three hairs stuck to her hand and she quickly flicked them away.

The man turned and walked to the Claims Department while she limped behind.

A half hour later, she and the tissue man were still standing in line, filling out forms. They finally completed the paperwork regarding the lost luggage, and with the airline's promise to deliver the bags as soon as they were located, they left the terminal.

Giving a pleasant nod, the man left. She turned to hail a cab and glanced up at the sky.

Maui weather was definitely better than Denver. Crystal blue skies, fluffy cumulus clouds drifting overhead. Taking a deep breath, she sniffed. Plumeria. The flower scented the tropical breeze with a heady perfume.

"Hello again," a voice sounded over Tess's shoulder.

She turned, as he tucked a brochure of some sort into the pocket of the coat he now carried draped over his arm.

He was back.

"Everything settled?" he said.

She nodded, glancing down at her snow boot that looked about as useless in the eighty-degree heat as a life preserver on a duck.

"Looks like that ankle's in bad shape—better have a doctor check it out as soon as you can." A taxi braked to the curb and the man opened the door. "This one's yours."

"No," she shook her head. "You take it."

"I insist." He held the door open wider.

"No, *I* insist."

"Look," he said. "You need to get ice on that ankle." He smiled. "Besides, if we don't decide soon, the cab will leave without either of us." A couple who stood ahead of them on the curb shot them dirty looks.

She said quietly, "I suppose we could share."

"Get in. I'll get your purse and briefcase," he offered.

"Thanks."

He positioned the items between them in the backseat, got in, and slammed the cab door.

"Where to?" the gum-chewing driver asked.

"Pioneer Inn for me," the man said.

She slid the man a peripheral glance and gave the driver Beeg's address.

Twenty minutes later, the driver braked at the front entrance of the historical Pioneer Inn, overlooking beautiful Lahaina Harbor. The tissue man stepped out of the cab and paid his fare.

Now this is more like it, she thought as she gazed around. Boats bobbed in the harbor, steel guitar music floated from the music stand on the corner. With a final wave, he said good-bye. Now she could get on with her vacation.

Forty minutes later, the cab wheeled back onto Wharf Street and deposited Tess at the Pioneer Inn. She had knocked and rung Beeg's doorbell for over ten minutes before a neighbor informed her that Ms. Harris was away.

Away.

What did he mean by "away"? Had she gone for a picnic at the other side of the island? The neighbor wasn't much help. "Just asked me to look after the place for a few days," the smallish man said.

Biting her lower lip, she had asked the neighbor to call another cab. Reasoning that she could call Beeg's cell phone once her luggage arrived with her address book, she decided to try the Pioneer Inn. It looked like a nice place, and she kind of liked the carved wooden captain she'd seen through the lobby windows.

She paid the fare and hauled her purse and briefcase out of the backseat, glad to be minutes away from a long soak in a hot tub. Ibuprofen and relaxation—the thought left her feeling giddy.

Tess emerged from the Pioneer Inn minutes later and lifted her hand for a cab. So much for lighted harbors in a beautiful historic setting. Unfortunately the driver was the one she'd left five minutes earlier. He smiled. "Back so soon?"

She heaved her purse and briefcase into the backseat and said simply, "No rooms."

The clerk called ahead to a place called the Mynah Nest. It was only six blocks away, and from the looks of it, it was rated down near the one-star range. Shutters hung askew from the windows, whose paint had peeled long before. The sign had a faded mynah bird painted on its top—the creature looked so worn it could've dropped from exhaustion alone. "Only one problem," the driver said over his shoulder.

She shut her eyes. "What?"

"The staff went out on strike two weeks ago."

She got out and paid her fare, mumbling an "I might call you back—we'll see," before shutting the door.

The place had a definite odor—and it wasn't plumeria. It had more of a rotten-egg quality. The carpet was a good decade past its last shampooing. The orange, rust, and brown design was dizzying, especially blurred by her inability to see it clearly. She walked up to the front desk, where she was met by a squeaky-voiced boy with hair that stood up at spiked angles. She wasn't sure if it was an intended 'do or not.

"Can I help you?" he asked.

"I heard your staff was on strike," she said.

"Yes, ma'am. I'm the manager here."

She raised a curious brow. "I guess I'd like a room."

"I can assure you that, despite the inconvenience of no staff, we will extend every effort to make your stay as comfortable as possible."

She nodded, squinting her eyes. He spoke like a professional. "Is there an optometrist close by?"

"Oh, yes, ma'am." She wished he'd stop calling her that. "There's all kinds of optical places in Maui." He wrote down an address for her.

"I'll need ice right away." She pointed toward her ankle. "And can you please phone the airport and inform them that I'm staying here? I have a couple of missing bags. I'd like them brought directly to my room the moment they arrive."

"Certainly, Ms. Nelson. Your room is 465. We hope you'll enjoy your stay."

The young manager handed her the key with a flourish, managing only to drop it at her feet. She bent painfully to retrieve it. At this point she didn't care if they put her on a sofa in the lobby, just so her foot was elevated and she had an ice pack and some aspirin.

"Where are the elevators?"

"Oh, sorry, ma'am." The freckle-faced boy flashed an embarrassed grin. "That's another tiny difficulty we're experiencing. The elevators are out of order right now—but we've called a repairman. He's due any minute. I'm sure he'll have those puppies up and running in a jif." His youthful features turned serious. "If you want to hang out in the lobby it's okay. There are house mints—they're free. You can have all you want."

She lifted a finger to her pounding temple. *Hang out in the lobby and eat house mints?* "No, thanks." Straightening, she reached for her purse and briefcase. "I'll take the stairs."

At least she didn't have two heavy pieces of luggage to tote.

She limped up four rickety flights, briefcase under one arm and her purse under the other. By the time she reached the fourth floor, she was wishing she'd joined a gym years earlier. Sagging against the plaster with sections of lathe peeking out from the peeled walls, she gasped to catch her breath. Her heartbeat had to be at least 265.

Working her way down the dimly lit hall, she followed the line of closed doors, squinting at the numbers. 465 was the room farthest from the stairway.

She unlocked the door, flicked on the lamp, and fell across the bed in exhaustion. Her ankle throbbed with every beat of her heart.

She lay on her back and studied the room. It sure wasn't fancy. The same rust, brown, and orange carpet lined the floors, and the bed had a padded vinyl "pillow" across its middle. She looked over toward the TV and noticed a pair of cowboy boots on the floor to the side. She wondered if the room had been cleaned. She shivered at the thought. Right now she didn't have the energy to deal with another crisis. By tomorrow she would connect with Beeg and this nightmare would be over.

She wondered how Len was managing without her. Would he realize how much she'd contributed to

Connor.com and want her back? She recalled Len's smug expression as he told her she was being replaced like an outdated pair of jeans. And what had she done? She'd limped away to lick her wounds like an injured pup.

Her mother would say she had gotten what she deserved. She had placed her trust in someone other than herself and that was never wise.

She'd been dismissed as if she hadn't sacrificed both private and work life to Connor.com these past five years.

The sun was sinking behind the strand of palms outside her window before she was able to convince herself to get up to check on what had happened to the ice bag the clerk had promised to deliver. "I've been washing sheets and I forgot," he said, then he apologized profusely and said he'd be up in a little while. She rolled off the side of the bed and limped into the bathroom. Minutes later, balanced on her good foot, steam floating around her, she anticipated the heavenly tub of hot water.

Suddenly there was a sharp rap at the door.

She groaned. "Just a minute."

The knock sounded again. "Keep your shirt on!" she called as she turned off the water and hobbled toward the door.

"Yes?" She stood and listened.

Silence.

She waited a few moments, then slid the security chain free and cautiously eased the door open. Sitting there were four pieces of scuffed black Samsonite with a bag of ice draped across the top.

"I can't believe this."

She had only two pieces of luggage missing. Not four. She stepped into the hall, hoping to catch the manager, but he was long gone.

She consulted the tag on the first and second bags and confirmed that the luggage was hers. The other two belonged to a Carter McConnell, whoever that was. Probably the guy from the airport, she surmised.

She sighed and dragged all four pieces into the room, then dropped the bag of ice into the sink and hobbled back to the bathroom. After her soak and a few minutes with ice on her ankle, she'd call the front desk and inform the clerk about the mix-up.

As far as she was concerned, if Mr. McConnell had been without his luggage this long, another hour wouldn't make any difference.

3

Tess slowly turned off the hot water with her big toe and lay back in a tub of hot salts as she let the steamy fragrance assuage her weary senses.

She hadn't thought that last week could be topped, but today had been worse. Beeg was missing; surely they were crisscrossing each other's path. Early tomorrow morning she would call Beeg's house, and if that effort failed to reach her, she would go to The Lopsided Easel, the small Front Street gallery where Beeg worked. They would share a cup of Kona coffee and have a good laugh about the whole thing—if she could remember how to laugh. She wiggled deeper into the hot suds.

As far as Connor.com—she'd let Len stew in his own juices for a few days. It wouldn't take a genius to discover that Tess Nelson contributed more to the company than Len ever dreamed. He would be calling her, begging her to come back; she'd bet the farm on that. She just needed to decide what her answer would be. Did she want to work for a man who could dismiss her with a wave of the hand? Didn't she have more self-respect than that?

Settling deeper into gardenia-scented water, she decided to wait a day or two before she checked her home messages. Then she would return to Connor.com on her own terms.

The delicious thought warmed her and made the last twenty-four hours tolerable.

Her fingers and toes had pruned and the water had cooled to chilly before she summoned enough energy to dry off and rub some fragrant cream on her skin. It felt so good to have her personal articles back. She'd recovered her glasses, cell phone, and address book, so she felt a measure of comfort.

Tightening her robe sash, she sat on the bed with her leg elevated on a pillow and the cool of the now-melting ice on her ankle. She stared at the two extra pieces of luggage beside the bed. Carter what's-his-name would probably appreciate having his items as much as she did. She needed to report the mistake.

The teenybopper manning the front desk answered her call in a piping little voice that harbored an adolescent crack.

"Yeah, what is it!"

"This is Tess Nelson in room 465. Two pieces of luggage have been delivered to my room by mistake."

"No joke?"

She rolled her eyes. "No joke. Would you please send up someone to get them?"

"Sure thing, lady. Do the bags have a name on 'em?"

"The tags say Carter McConnell."

"McConnell, McConnell—" The young man repeated the name under his breath. Tess could hear him frantically rummaging through some papers.

"Yeah, here ya go—Carter McConnell. He just checked in—he's in room 464. Just down the hall from you. Uh, sorry 'bout the mix-up there, lady. Tell ya what I'm gonna do. Soon as I can get a few minutes I'll hop on up there to get 'em."

Good grief. She looked at her melted bag of ice and thought of the hour she'd already wasted and knew Mr. McConnell would want to have his personal effects as soon as possible.

"If it isn't against hotel policy, perhaps I could just set Mr. McConnell's luggage outside his door?"

"If you don't think it's too much hassle . . . hop to it."

"Okay, I'll take care of it."

"Thanks a wad, lady," he said, then hung up.

She gingerly placed her weight on her injured

ankle. She was pleased to note it didn't hurt as much as before, although it had taken on numbness. Adding a fraction more bulk, she flinched and nearly fell.

She scooted the pieces of luggage to the door. Talk about weight! The man must have packed bricks in one of the bags.

Shoving the bags into the hall, she wondered if knocking and leaving them in front of the door of room 464 would be sufficient. That was the way the bags had been delivered to her. But, she reasoned, if the man weren't there the bags might be stolen before he returned to his room.

She tapped lightly on the door, then allowed ample time for the man to respond. When there was no response, she knocked, louder this time.

What idiot was knocking on the door?

Carter rolled over onto his back and opened his eyes, trying to remember where he was. The antihistamines he'd taken had his thinking process on the blink. The mix-up at Pioneer Inn, thinking he had a room only to discover that his reservation had been eaten by the computer and he couldn't get a room until tomorrow night, then the frantic search for another room, and being reduced to a stay in the Mynah Nest, was enough to throw him off balance. He'd wanted to get settled, start the relaxing process. It would be another day before he could get in to the Pioneer Inn.

The persistent knock rattled him.

He couldn't remember the last time he'd felt so worn out. Now some nincompoop was trying to beat down the door.

Annoyed, he rolled out of bed as whoever it was pounded on the door again. He stumbled, bumping his knee on the desk, and finally reached the door, but not before his big toe found a straight pin some former guest had dropped on the carpeted floor.

Pain shot up his calf, and he sucked in a breath as he dropped to his knees to extract the blasted harpoon. The slight trickle of blood when he pulled the pin free made him sick to his stomach. He was a lily-livered coward when it came to the sight of blood, especially his own.

Another brisk knock on the door brought him back to his feet.

"Okay! Okay! I'm coming!" Hopping on one foot, he slid the security chain free and cracked the door a fraction.

Oh, great. The wren. What was *she* doing here? And in a bathrobe? He averted his gaze to the floor.

"Mr. McConnell? I'm sorry to bother you but—"

Carter opened the door wider and Tess stepped back, clearly startled. They stared at each other. Finally Carter prompted. "How did you find me here? Are you following me?"

She stood speechless. Her lips moved but no sound came out. "You're Carter McConnell?" He nodded his head.

"How dare you!" she sputtered. "I am not the kind of person who follows total strangers! Besides, you were staying at the Pioneer Inn."

He leaned on the doorsill, still fighting sleep. "I *thought* I was staying at the Pioneer Inn. Some mix-up with the reservations—computer glitch. I move to the Pioneer tomorrow night." He yawned, running his hand through his tousled hair. "So, what do you want if you're not stalking me?"

"The airline delivered your bags to my room by mistake—I thought you'd want to have them right away. Of course, I wouldn't have disturbed you had I known . . ."

He glanced from the towel on her head down to her bare feet. Her left ankle and foot looked like an over-inflated water balloon. "That's looking worse." He pointed at her foot. "What was your name?"

"Tess Nelson," she spurted. "And I'll thank you to mind your own business." She turned and marched toward her room. Carter tugged his luggage into his room and then dropped across the bed and fell asleep before he could think another thought.

4

"Looks like that storm is intensifying, Erin," the radio announcer began. Tess lifted her head to see what time it was—7:12. "The meteorologists are picking out names as this baby grows, with sustained winds up to fifty miles per hour. We're on standby here in Maui but who knows if she'll change directions."

She turned off the alarm. So much for sleeping in today. If she were home she'd already be on her snack break. She stuffed the thought aside. She was on vacation. She was going to enjoy.

As she stepped out of bed the pain in her foot surged. She needed to find a doctor and see about getting a contact lens, but not before she got ahold of Beeg.

Picking up her cell phone and address book she called Beeg's home number again. The answering machine picked up. When it beeped, Tess said, "Hey,

Beeg, I'm here in Maui, but I seem to keep missing you. Call me on my cell phone." She hung up and stared at her phone. Where could Beeg be? It wasn't as if she didn't expect her to come.

Padding to the bathroom, she brushed her teeth and then took out a brush and started in on her hair. A big clump of hair dropped into the sink. She looked at it in disgust. She'd have to wear a hat today, definitely.

This is not my idea of the perfect vacation. Tess exited the hotel in search of an eye and foot doctor. She'd decided to stop back at the airport to rent a car too, since she hadn't gotten ahold of Beeg and taking taxis everywhere was getting quite costly.

Once that was taken care of, it was time to attend to her injuries. Her ankle now looked like a bloated corpse, and the sprain needed a doctor's attention.

Thirty minutes later she was sitting in a clinic, fanning herself with a coverless issue of *People* magazine—recently and thoroughly mangled by the four-year-old sitting next to her.

A nurse appeared through an outer door. "Ms. Nelson?"

"Me." Tess laid the magazine aside and stood up and hobbled to follow the white uniform. Upon entering examining room four, she was sat on a narrow table with a long strip of white paper where the nurse efficiently recorded her blood pressure and temperature. Stripping the sphygmomanometer off, she then scribbled notes before positioning a clipboard on her trim stomach. "What can we do for you today?"

"I sprained my ankle running to catch a plane. It's very painful."

She nodded. "Visiting Hawaii?"

"Yes."

She clipped the pencil on the board. "Doctor will be in shortly." The door closed behind her, and Tess drew a deep breath, holding her foot out in front of her to reassess the damage. The ankle was blue and distorted—could she have chipped the bone? The prospect added another unwelcome angst to her growing list.

Thirty minutes later, the doctor appeared. Tess sat up quickly; she'd finally given in to the uncomfortable table and laid back. Absently smoothing her hair, she smiled at the gray-haired physician with a noticeable paunch.

He peered at the chart in his hand. "Having ankle problems?"

"I sprained it while I was running to catch a plane. It's been throbbing for hours."

"Hummm." Setting the chart aside, he took her bare foot and examined it.

"Yes . . . hummm. There's considerable swelling and bruising."

"I've taken Advil and used ice packs but nothing helps." She waited, heart pumping erratically. What if it was broken and she had to endure a hot cast—which would undoubtedly mean crutches. . . . Her heart banged against her rib cage.

"Humm . . ." He bent closer and carefully manipulated the smarting appendage. Tess gritted her teeth and closed her eyes.

"Hurt?"

Pain! Searing agony, you masochist!

She grinned. "A little."

"Hummm." Straightening, his eyes focused on a mole on her left arm. Narrowing in on the site, he examined the barely distinguishable discoloration. "How long have you had this?"

The heart again. Thumping wildly, crowding the back of her throat. "All my life—I think." She tried to remember—she'd had the mole all her life, hadn't she? The blemish looked vaguely familiar—but maybe it had come up lately. She felt faint.

"Does it look strange? *Dangerous?*" She turned to

peer at the now definitely suspicious looking *thing* on her left forearm.

"Hummm." He pulled a light over to the table, switched it on, then reached for a magnifying glass. Wide-eyed, she studied his grave demeanor, ankle forgotten. Drawing the light nearer, he scoured the object for what seemed an inordinately long time.

"What?" she asked faintly.

"Hummm . . ." The magnifying glass moved back and forth—an inch here, half inch there. . . .

Sweat broke out on her forehead.

Straightening, he snapped off the light and pushed the stand back. "I'm going to write you a prescription for pain and something to relax those muscles. Before you leave I'd like to take an X-ray of that foot, but I believe we're dealing with a simple sprain."

Nodding mutely, she tried to fathom how pain and muscle relaxants could relate to a suspicious looking mole? Dear God—she'd *never* noticed. Len had thrown her into such a tailspin, and she'd been so busy with work. . . . Had she overlooked something? Melanoma. She'd read article after article about the dreaded skin condition. She lifted her forearm and stared.

The doctor wrote on the pad. Her mind faintly registered the scrape of ball point against paper. She'd have to fly home immediately—consult her doctor, who would then refer her to a specialist. How good were Denver oncologists? Her hands trembled. She would fly to the Mayo Clinic in Rochester, Minnesota—she'd have the best of care there— maybe even extend her life a few more years. . . . Her heart sank. There was so much yet to do—so many things she'd wanted to experience. Motherhood. She wanted to spend a summer in Ireland, take an Alaskan cruise.

"I'll wrap the ankle—should give you some relief," the doctor was saying. He tore the prescription off the pad. "You call the office tomorrow and my nurse will give you the results of the X-ray. Meanwhile," he smiled, "enjoy our beautiful island."

She nodded, numb now. "The . . . mole. Should I see . . . ?"

"The mole?" He flapped the air. "Perfectly normal. You've probably had it all your life." He turned and walked out, closing the door behind him.

Weakly lowering herself flat on her back, she stared at the ceiling, trying to still her racing heart.

An hour later and two blocks away, Tess walked through the door of an optical service whose flashing red sign promised, "Ready in one hour." *Now to get rid of these glasses.*

For the next hour and a half, she read magazines and filed her nails. One whole morning in paradise shot on medical emergencies, plus the visits cost twice what she'd have paid on the Mainland.

"Ms. Nelson?"

Tess tossed the magazine aside and for the second time that morning hobbled into a small cubicle—this one filled with strange looking apparatus for a preliminary exam. She read numbers, pointed right and left, and pushed a button each time a flash occurred.

She jumped when a blast of air hit her right eye: glaucoma test. Moments later she was ushered into the optician's chair. When the man entered, she did a double take at his bottle-thick lenses, which he repeatedly shoved to the bridge of his nose with his forefinger.

"Lost a contact?"

"In the airport."

"Shame." Up went the glasses. After a series of tests—ptosis, exophthalmos, lesions, deformities or asymmetry problems—he got down to the business at hand.

She heard a flipping sound. "Is A better, or B?" the doctor asked.

"B."

She heard a click. "B or A?" Up went the glasses.

"A."

Click. "A or B?"

"Uh . . . A—no wait. Let me see B again."

Click.

"What was the question?"

"A or B." Up went the glasses.

"B. No, A."

"A or B?"

"A."

She was getting dizzy.

Click. "B or A?"

"B—A—I don't know. They both look the same."

Twenty minutes later she walked out, after paying for the examination and ordering one contact, which she now had to kill an hour before she could get. She settled on lunch and a brief excursion through a trendy dress shop where she purchased a silk blouse for an outlandish price. All in all, she considered the morning had cost her close to three hundred dollars, and it was barely noon.

Breezing out of the optometrist shop, she smiled, relieved to be free of the annoying glasses. Her foot hit something sticky on the sidewalk, and she paused and lifted her heel, groaning when she saw a wad of pink bubble gum stuck to the leather sole. Lowering the good foot, she scraped back and forth, keeping an eye out for curious bystanders. Her sandaled foot moved back and forth, back and forth, each rub producing nothing more than a long, stringy, sticky piece of gum-based latex.

Sun glared down on her, and she felt perspiration running down her neck. Her wrapped ankle throbbed. The gum was stuck as tight as an eight-day clock. She could remove the shoe, but walking barefoot on the warm pavement didn't interest her—not when she had to shuffle anyway. She'd have to make it back to the car and get rid of the sandal.

With a goal fixed in mind, she limped down the concrete, trailing a long, gooey slick of pink bubble gum on the hot pavement.

This vacation was going nowhere but to the dogs.

With her health care needs dealt with, Tess decided to walk to Beeg's gallery near the historical Baldwin Missionary Home. She crossed the street and stopped to gawk at the Banyon tree in the middle of a small park where craft vendors peddled their wares. The tree branches spread for blocks.

"Something, isn't it?" a voice said.

She turned to see a nicely dressed woman sitting on a bench, smiling at her. She wore her iron gray hair braided and looped in a coronet. Even sitting on a rustic bench, her posture and the way she held her head appeared almost queenly. Her eyes, blue as Hawaiian skies, were warm and alert, expressing a friendly interest. A native woven basket containing cut plumeria and birds-of-paradise sat next to a shopping bag. Tess glanced at a loaf of fresh baked bread and a carton of milk in the shopping bag.

"The tree was planted by the sheriff of Maui in 1873 and is now the largest in the state," the woman offered.

"It is amazing." She turned back to study the tourist attraction. Where the tree's roots thickened, they formed a series of columns like tendons in the tree's neck to support the ever-lengthening branches.

"Ficus benghalensis," the lady said in explanation. "The tree now stands nearly sixty feet tall and covers more than two-thirds of an acre." Her timeless features softened as she stared up at the sun filtering lacey fingers through the branches. "One of God's many marvels."

Tess smiled and moved on. *God's marvels.*

She'd never thought of it that way.

Trekking by ocean-front stores, she spotted the Lopsided Easel half a block away. The small upstairs gallery looked inviting with its colorful array of watercolors decorating the window. She paused to read the list of artists represented there; of course Beeg as well as other talents like Don Jusko, Michael Krahan, and Jim Kingwell, who was noted for his watercolors of local scenes.

She entered the store, alive with color, space, and movement, and smiled at the pretty young Polynesian girl behind the counter. "Hi," she said. "Tell Bee Gee her past has come back to haunt her."

New York City.

Bee Gee had gone to the Mainland for an art showing and she'd be gone two weeks! She vaguely remembered Beeg saying something about New York. She wanted to pull her hair in sheer frustration. But she knew with the state her hair was in that it wouldn't be wise. The clerk at the gallery had given her the Marriott number where Beeg was staying, but what good would it do to call? Beeg was in New York and she was in Maui.

After she'd left the Lopsided Easel, she had aimlessly wandered the streets of Lahaina, trying to gain control of her emotions. A cacophony of tropical bird calls and Don Ho's voice blared from street corner vendors' stereos.

Now what? Should she book the next flight back to Denver or stay in Hawaii and force herself to enjoy her time off?

She needed aspirin.

Depressed, she drove back to the Mynah Nest. The foul odor of rotten eggs met her again. Well, Tess decided, the least she could do was find a nicer place to stay. She drove to the Pioneer Inn where the clerk assured her there were now open rooms.

When the clerk gave her the key to her room she smiled and made her way up. This room was markedly cleaner and smelled fresh. Still, Beeg was gone. She had no one to share her time with. She hung the "Do Not Disturb" sign on the door and then did exactly what she promised herself she wouldn't: she called home to check her messages. She had a three o'clock dental appointment on Monday that she'd forgotten to cancel. The jewelry store had the broken locket fixed. She could pick it up anytime.

She downed two aspirins and went to bed.

5

In spite of the pending tropical storm which, according to the weather bureau, had just kicked up another notch, she was determined to start her vacation. The travel brochure she had picked up in the Pioneer Inn lobby claimed that there was nowhere on earth more beautiful to witness at sunrise than the summit of Mount Haleakala. Her ankle was stronger this morning so she rented a car, purchased a latte, and made the two-hour drive to the crater and the short hobble to the summit. As she watched, the blazing ball eased up over the dormant volcano crater, radiant light gradually spreading until it infused the sky with brilliant golds and yellows. It was the most glorious thing she had ever seen. On her drive home, she was still affected by it, almost as if it were a religious experience, as if she'd somehow seen a bit of God in that sunrise.

She knew she was far from spiritual. She thought about the times her grandmother had taken her to Mass when she was a child. It held the same sense of reverence and hushed awe. Mom, of course, didn't like priests, or the church.

"Religion gives outgoing folks something to do on Sunday mornings. But really—God? You're smarter than that, Tess."

"But, Mom," Tess had said. *"The nice woman in the black robe and funny-looking thing on her head—that 'Sister'—she says there is a God, and that He loves little children."*

"And there's a pot of gold at the end of the rainbow!"

Tess hadn't known what to think. She'd wanted to believe in a God who cared about her, but as she'd grown older she'd seen too little of such kindness, especially with people like Len Connor. She felt more and more certain that her mother was right.

As Tess drove into Maui, she felt as though she was marooned on the moon.

Restless now, she decided to ignore her smarting ankle and do *something*. Food. She needed a decent meal to put events in perspective, to put her life into perspective. When she asked where she could find a good meal, the concierge suggested a luau—the Old Lahaina Luau located within easy walking distance of Pioneer Inn. She had been thinking more along the lines of swordfish and salad at the grill below the hotel, but maybe a little entertainment would jump-start the vacation mode.

Returning upstairs, she dressed in a pair of white walking shorts and a butter-yellow T-shirt and pulled her hair atop her head and stuffed it into her hat. Slipping on a pair of sandals, which looked awful with the injured ankle wrapped, she went back downstairs and exited the hotel.

The air outside was scented with tuberose and jasmine—or so she tried to imagine—after all this was "paradise." Actually the scent of hamburger from that cheeseburger joint a couple blocks away accompanied her as she took her time walking to the luau. Gusty winds had slackened to a nice breeze though the evening was slightly overcast.

The luau grounds were typical native Hawaiian. Palm trees, grass huts, and steel guitars blended to create an authentic setting. A handsome Polynesian young man wearing a brightly flowered *tupenu* smiled as he looped an orchid lei over her head. Her mood lightened as she accepted a glass of fruit punch with a fresh orchid floating in it. Demonstrations of lei making, coconut cutting, and Ti leaf shirt weaving lined the walkways. She wandered the grounds, sipping her drink.

After posing for the required souvenir picture with said Polynesian hunk, Tess was directed to her seat. As she approached her chair, she did a quick double take. Sitting at the same table, binoculars lifted as he studied the bobbing boats in the harbor, sat none other than Carter McConnell. When he lifted his eyes and saw her, disbelief crossed his face. She set her drink on the table and sat down. "Now who's stalking whom?"

"Nice to see you again, too."

She glanced at the binoculars as he held them aloft. "Thirty-nine fifty. Hilo Hattie's," he said in explanation. "Want to look?" He held them up for her.

"No," she said as a gust of wind lifted her hat. She quickly pulled it back down, shoving it tightly onto her head.

A pair of lovely Polynesian girls came by, grass skirts rustling. "Would you two like a hula lesson?"

She looked over at Carter's face, which had turned a dark shade of pink. "Uh," he stammered. "No thanks." One of the girls wiggled her hips and made a waving motion in front of herself with her arms. "It's not hard," she encouraged. "I bet your wife would love to get a picture of you doing it."

Now it was her turn to blush. She felt the heat rise up her cheeks.

The second girl pulled Carter to his feet and positioned his hands in front of him, showing him the foot movement. "This is the Ami'ami," she explained. "Now move your hips back and forth." Carter jerked around like a marionette on a string. "No, it's a smaller movement, a little jiggle like this." She demonstrated. Tess swallowed back her amusement as he let the girls make a fool of out him.

When Carter spotted Tess's growing jollity, he leaned over and said something to one of the women. Smiling, they hula-ed over, hips gyrating wildly as they drew a protesting Tess into the act.

"My ankle," she objected.

Carter grinned. "If you can walk on it, you can dance. Come on, give it a try."

The women positioned her next to Carter, draped a grass shirt around her trim hips, and showed her the proper movements. At first she felt conspicuous, but soon she was gyrating along with the others. The four *Akalewa* swayed their hips from side to side, in a graceful interpretation of the native art, *Ha'a*. Tess figured the hand movements were beyond her, but she could swing a grass skirt with the best of them.

"A new talent to wow the homefolks," Carter said.

"I can just imagine doing this at a board meeting." She laughed and tried to mimic the hand movements, which looked easy and graceful, but somehow didn't translate well when she tried them.

"Just what a flight controller needs: hula proficiency." He exaggerated a gyration. "I'll add it to my resume."

The crowd watched, laughing at the playful antics. Before Tess realized it she was actually having fun.

By the time they made their way back to the table she was glad for the reprieve. "I haven't moved like that since my last junior high dance," Carter said.

"What about senior high?" she teased.

"I gave up dancing." There was a twinkle in his eyes that she hadn't noticed before. "What about you?" he said.

"I did the ballet thing for a while. At least until my ballet teacher told me to take up football. I never caught on." They shared a chuckle.

"It looks like they're pulling the pig out of the pit," Carter said. "Want to go watch?"

They stood side by side as the animal with the apple in its mouth was lifted onto the main serving table.

"Where I come from, you don't bury a pig and then dig him back up and eat him," she told him. He grinned.

After they had filled their plates, she noticed that he briefly bowed his head before he ate. Praying, she supposed. He didn't seem like one of those religious fanatics who said, "Bless this and bless that." She made a note to ask him about it later.

The food, pork included, was surprisingly delicious: Lomi Lomi Salmon, Pulehue Steak, Guava Chicken, Haupia, otherwise known as coconut pudding, banana bread, Taro Rolls, Poi, and Kalua Pua's.

"That's free-range pork," Carter supplied after consulting the menu.

They looked at each other and repeated in unison: "The pig."

"How can a pig be free-range anyhow?" Carter leaned over and whispered. "Was it raised in its natural environment? And where would *that* be?" Tess laughed and looked at him. He sure seemed different than the grumpy guy whose luggage she'd delivered the day before. But then she'd been pretty exhausted too, so she guessed she could understand the change. He was an easy person to be around.

By the time the entertainment began she felt relaxed and happy. They applauded the performance of the beautiful ancient hula Kahiko and 'Auana. For the first time since she'd arrived in Hawaii she felt as though everything was going to be all right. She couldn't say why, exactly. Nothing had changed. She was still without a job. Maybe it was making a new friend.

The wind tossed the dancer's hair, and Tess pulled her hat down tighter.

Cramming a piece of roll into his mouth, Carter applauded. Then leaning over he asked, "Is it supposed to rain?" He tilted his head toward the sky that had taken on a starless appearance. The wind kicked up again.

She shrugged. She'd heard Beeg mention that rain showers were frequent on this side of the island so she wouldn't be surprised—though the cool feel in the air hinted at something stronger than a tropical mist. She studied Carter's relaxed manner. Like her, he was wearing a flower lei some Polynesian lovely had draped over his head. He was smiling, having a great time in spite of their rocky beginning.

"Nice, huh?" he said, laugh crinkles forming around friendly blue eyes.

She nodded. The luau was therapeutic, a sorely needed diversion from a hectic past few days.

She looked up. The wind was whipping across the lawn so strongly that the dancers were having trouble keeping their balance; costumes were wrapping around their bodies, and the girls' long black hair flailed around their faces, making it hard for them to see. A gale whistled through the musicians' microphones, sending an ear-piercing shriek of feedback.

Servers darted about to set desserts—Haupia pudding, Haupia cake, pineapple upside-down cake, guava cake, and coffee—in front of the guests before the full gale hit. Tess leaned to cut a slice of pineapple upside-down cake when the wind whipped a glob of brown sugar into the hair of the woman two chairs down. The woman gave her a dirty look and then left in a huff.

Thunder grumbled. Guests dressed in flimsy island wear clasped their forearms in an attempt to keep warm, teeth chattering as the skies opened up. Waiters and waitresses rushed to rescue the food, pulling out carts they quickly loaded with platters and took inside. Waiters handed out flimsy yellow plastic rain ponchos and guests tried to wrestle the gear over their heads in the whipping wind.

"Are we having fun yet?" Cater shouted into the wind.

"A blast!" Tess replied. "Help me put this on." Carter reached over, but the wind persisted, making it impossible to find the narrow slits in the sides.

Chairs overturned. The entertainers courageously

plowed ahead on the semi-circular stage below as Poi-logged spectators made for higher ground. Rain sluiced down, but the musicians bravely played on.

". . . the missionaries brought many changes to our island," the announcer intoned. *Shreeeek, shrill-lll*, the reverb sounded.

". . . King Kalakaua . . . Drat!" The announcer flung the mike to the ground as lightning forked the arena.

"Let's get out of here!" Carter took her hand and the two ran-hobbled toward the lobby's thatched roof. "Are you okay?" Carter released her hand and looked at her drenched face.

"I'm fine," Tess said. "Wet. But fine." She looked down at her feet; the foot without injury had a broken sandal strap.

"Rats!" She said. "Now I need to go sandal shopping, since this is the only pair I brought."

"You need an excuse to shop?" It was a question.

"That's a stereotype, I'll have you know. Not all women love spending money."

"I didn't mean it as an affront." Carter held up both hands and smiled. "Truce?"

She blushed. "Truce."

"Let me hail a cab," Carter offered.

"Are you all right?" he asked again as he helped

her into the backseat when a taxi finally pulled up. Water streamed off her chin in rivulets. *How can he be so calm?* she thought.

"Fine. I just want to get into dry clothes."

6

She wasn't about to let bad luck get her down, Tess decided the next morning when she woke up.

Dazzling sunlight filtered through the window as she lifted a slat to look out. Paradise shimmered like a priceless jewel in the rain-drenched harbor. *Papahanaumoku*—Earth Mother—as the emcee had called it last night, looked to be in a better mood this morning. And so was she. Smiling, she dropped the louver back into place.

Her thoughts drifted to Denver. She was tired of wondering what was happening at Connor.com. Len Connor could take a flying leap; Chuck Somebody could wrestle with hiring, resource allocation, compensation, benefits, and compliance with OSHA laws. After an eighteen-hour day manning the phones and handling Connor.com's problems, the "good ol' boys" could kick back, have a beer, and try to figure out the mess.

Tess wasn't going to lift a finger to help. The thought was liberating.

She stared at her reflection in the mirror. A tan—she needed one of those billboard browns that would be the envy of every woman in Denver. She wanted to look her loveliest when she spooned crow onto Len Connor's plate.

After eating pineapple and cinnamon toast at the grill, Tess then headed to Makena Big Beach with a new umbrella and a bottle of Maui Baby, Maui Island's Secret Browning Formula. She'd bought a beach chair, too.

She braked in the public asphalt parking lot and hauled the newly purchased items out of the trunk. By the time she got to the beach, the shoreline was already swarming with scantily clad men and women as they staggered beneath the weight of overloaded backpacks, boogie boards, and snorkel paraphernalia.

After turning the beach umbrella just so, she reached for the tanning lotion and peeled out of her turquoise and hot pink Hawaiian-print sarong. What she'd do with the superfluous piece of clothing in Denver she didn't know. Pretzeling herself into the chair, she began applying the lotion, then leaned back and relaxed behind oversized sunglasses, prepared to spend a leisurely morning. Lazy wavelets of aquamarine water lapped against the shoreline. Feathered fans of palm leaves wove a dark tracery against a sky so blue it made her heart ache. A gentle breeze brought the tang of sea salt mixed with the intoxicating aroma of flowers. An exotic blended fragrance not found in a bottle.

She wondered what Connor.com peons were doing. Slaving away over copy machines, no doubt, staring numb-minded at blinking cursors and answering ringing phones.

She sighed. She missed it. Missed the hassle, the adrenaline rush—really missed it. But she wondered, was that the meaning of life? To slave away at a job she got no recognition for? Or worse, for just a paycheck. Wasn't there supposed to be a deeper meaning in all of this?

The sun beat down. The sound of laughing children's voices drifted toward her. The kids were building a sandcastle on the beach. Children. Precious little miracles. Would she ever have any of her own? She'd been so busy building a career that she had never really paused to consider the question. Thirty-two wasn't ancient, but she could hear her biological clock ticking—or was that the idiot's rap music, farther down the beach, blaring in her ear?

Lazily warm, she dozed, opening her eyes occasionally when she heard the excited cries of a beachcomber who'd spotted a whale frolicking near one of the islands jutting out of the water. *Big whoop,* she thought irritably.

Suddenly the wind shifted. Sand kicked up—instantly coating the Maui Baby tanning lotion in a grainy sheet.

She sat up, shielding her eyes as sunbathers started to race past her. Big Beach had suddenly turned into the Sahara Desert with a sandstorm approaching. The wind machine gunned gritty pellets at unsuspecting sun-worshipers.

Spitting sand, she sprang up and grabbed the umbrella. Wind caught the frame and stripped the fabric inside out. Another hefty gust sent her nearly airborne as she stumbled around, trying to wedge her toes into a pair of rubber flip-flops. "Stupid thongs!" she muttered. Sun-blistered snorkelers boiled out of the churning water to make a dash for the shoreline.

Grabbing her belongings, she set off for the car. Her hat blew off and she went to retrieve it. The injured ankle gave way then, and she stumbled, then pulled herself upright before she hobbled on.

Ramming what was left of the shredded umbrella into the nearest trash receptacle, she lunged for the car. Once inside, she dug sand out of her eyes and ears and places where sand didn't belong.

Grasping hold of the steering wheel, she batted her forehead against the backs of her hands. *Why-why-why?* Why *couldn't* she have a nice relaxing vacation?

After a moment, her nerves calmed. A shower. She needed a shower to get rid of this sand. She turned the key in the ignition . . . and heard nothing.

Nothing.

She whacked the steering wheel. "Don't do this!"

She turned the key again.

Nothing.

"No. *No.*" Gritting her teeth, she tried again. Grinding. Grinding.

Again.

Nothing. Grind.

Clamping her eyes shut, she heaved an exacerbated *oooomph.* Faced with the inevitable, she fumbled in her purse for her cell phone.

Grimacing against the feel of gritty sand in uncomfortable places, she listened for the dial tone and found she had none. Of course. *Tess, you're losing it, girl. Okay.* She looked around, deciding she had to take charge of the situation. Sand still pitted the car's windows. Who knew how long this would keep up? She'd just have to borrow a cell phone from a fellow sun-worshiper. So, pulling her hat down on her head and retying the sarong around her waist, she opened the car door and began to make her way in the wind and sand to a phone. The back of her sand-logged swimsuit hung a good two inches too low as she walked backward through the gale, trying to avoid getting more grit in her eyes. "Hey!" a voice said as she felt a thump against her back. "Watch where you're going, lady!" a tall, tanned Adonis said in a gruff voice.

Her face flamed. "Sorry. Can I use your cell phone?" And for once, the man had one. Her luck was picking up.

"I don't *know* what's wrong with the car," she told the rental agent. "It won't start. I turn the key and nothing happens."

"We'll send someone right away—Big Beach, right?"

"Right." Big *sandy* beach. The clerk didn't mention that help was still two hours away.

And so as the sun set on Lahaina Harbor on Tess Nelson's third night in paradise, she was in her room, soaking a sprained ankle and trying to get the taste of sand out of her mouth. Too weary to eat, she skipped dinner and fell asleep before eleven, only to be awakened by the wind around three a.m. Peering out the window blinds, she watched palms bending to the onslaught, loose fronds whipping across the parking lot.

"Gilligan's Island," she conceded. "I'm trapped on Gilligan's Island."

What would Mona think of her now?

"She's so pretty." Tess stared at the beautiful creature lying in a pink velvet box. Its blue eyes opened and closed, and when she pressed its tummy, the baby cried real tears. She never cried. Mona spanked her when she cried.

"Please, Mommy. Can't I have this doll?"

"Oh, all right, you ungrateful twit. You can have the stupid doll. I hope you're happy."

Mona glared at her daughter as she paid for the purchase. They left the store and got into the car to go home. But before Mona turned on the ignition, she looked at the doll and said snidely, "It looks like it's lying in a coffin."

Tess felt her heart drop. Why did her mother have to spoil everything?

She lowered the window blind. What had made her think about Mona and that silly doll? Unpleasant events of the past few days? It wasn't as if she didn't have dolls—but that one was special—a child's delight.

Other girls at school—girls with pretty clothes and Beaver Cleaver mothers—sailed through life on a magic carpet. Their mothers had pretty polished nails; Mona's hands were rough from factory work and they perpetually smelled of cigarette smoke. Other girls' moms came to PTA and were room mothers who visited school on holidays and birthdays bearing pretty plates of cupcakes and cookies.

Mona never came to anything. She didn't have time to bake cupcakes and cookies or be a room mother. Once she promised she would, but she hadn't. Only recently had it occurred to her that Mona had had to work—the family needed two incomes to survive. Maybe if Mona had talked to Tess about it, she might have understood, maybe even accepted the fact that not everyone lived the ideal family lifestyle.

Still, her mother and father were forever making promises to go to the movies or get ice cream, but when the time came they were too tired. She had vowed to herself that when she grew up, she would take care of herself. She'd eat all the ice cream and go to all the movies she wanted. She might even make enough money to buy a movie theatre and be the envy of every girl in class. She'd have a home with good furniture, not some old pieces of junk from the thrift store, and she'd buy it all with her own money that she'd work hard for, and no one would ever take it away from her because she was tough—even though sometimes it hurt to be tough.

On Sunday mornings she'd watch her friends, all dressed up in their nice clothes as they drove away to church with their PTA mothers and Ward Cleaver fathers. She imagined the happy families coming back to eat pot roast and mashed potatoes and gravy, sitting at a table with pretty plates and saucers and even fresh flowers, and she'd wonder why, if there were a God, did He love some people more than He did others? Because it was obvious that He did.

"Your problem is that you're too trusting, Tess," Mona said. A cigarette dangled from the corner of her mouth, and the stench of smoke filled the room. "You need to grow up," she said. "Now come away from that window. Those folks are putting on airs. Jack Pierson may look like the perfect husband and father, but I know for a fact Jack likes his brandy. Don't be fooled by people. Do you really think anything in this life is that perfect?—that trusting in some mystical God to run your life is going to keep you from having troubles? Now set

the table for breakfast and maybe we'll all go for a ride later."

"Promise?"

"Promise."

Mona was right. She had let down her guard and placed her trust in Len Connor. And Len had shafted her big time.

I'm hiring a fraternity brother. But there's that position in payroll . . .

Mona would give her an earful when she heard that she had been demoted—fired, whatever. She should call her, but they rarely talked. Guilt nagged her when she thought of how little time she allotted family—but then the Nelson family gave a whole new definition to "family."

She picked up a travel brochure and leafed through the pages. A drive to Hana promised spectacular waterfalls and freshwater pools. Hawaiian "cattle country." African tulip trees, towering Baldwin pines, colorful exotic plants and flowers, the variegated greens of the endless tropical scenery—none of which really interested her. At least not right now.

Wadding the paper, she threw it aside and started to pace. She hated this feeling, this panicky feeling of not knowing what was going to happen next. Fear of the unknown set her teeth on edge. Maybe she'd been wrong to leave. Maybe she should go back and fight for her job. If she stayed and waited for Len, would he ever recognize his mistake? Suddenly she felt overwhelmed, as though she were drowning. A headache bloomed at the base of her skull.

7

Sitting at the small table in her room, Tess casually leafed through "Driving Maui" while she finished breakfast. Her eye caught the "Whale Watch" excursion. Humpbacks migrated from the North Pacific to Maui's southern and western shores during late November through March to mate, calve, and nurse their young in warm Hawaiian waters.

Whales. Well, why not. She wished she didn't have to go alone. Her thoughts turned to that man she'd spent time with at the luau and she wondered what he was doing today. Then just as quickly, she tossed the idea aside.

Donning a pair of shorts, a T-shirt, and flip-flops, she reached for her sunglasses, binoculars (thanks to Hilo Hattie's), and sunscreen, and looked at her reflection in the mirror. Was that a bald spot near her left temple? She moved closer to see, running her hand through the strands, a few of which came loose and clung to her fingers. "Great!" she murmured. Nerves had her going bald. Great. She grabbed a bandanna and tied it securely around her head, then left for the wharf to purchase a ticket.

Captain Commando Humpback Whale Picture Patrol—a certified thirteen-passenger inflatable boat—bobbed at its mooring.

Water, wind, and surf. She climbed aboard and leaned back as the captain set out to sea. The boat skimmed foamy waves. She gazed at the immensity of it all. Hadn't she heard somewhere that God showed Himself in nature? She wondered if even God was surprised by His handiwork the day He formed the oceans.

No, she supposed. Nothing surprised Him, not even the beauty she saw this morning.

So, ol' girl, why can't you let go and let God handle the rough spots in your life? If He's smart enough to create all you see, maybe He's big enough to oversee your piddling crisis. Name me one man or woman who doesn't have problems, but the wise soul doesn't fool himself into thinking he controls it. But she'd been in charge of her life for so long she didn't know how to even begin.

A couple of miles offshore, the captain stopped the boat. "We got to be quiet and watch," the overweight man with the standard captain's hat said, finger to lips. The other ten tourists gazed with hushed awe, turning in circles to see who would be first to spot their prey.

After a few minutes a teenage boy with bright red hair pointed as he squeaked, "Thar she blows!" The excited tourists heaved to portside, causing the raft to shift. Men, children, and women jostled for position, binoculars to their eyes, shouting, "Portside!" then, "Starboard!" pointing out each sighting.

It wasn't long before she tired of trying to catch a glimpse. She moved to the back bench. She'd stuffed a novel in her backpack; she'd read and leave the whales their privacy.

Sitting back, she opened the book and yawned. Sun reflected off the water and made her drowsy. Tess closed her eyes and soaked up the rays.

A second later they snapped open in time to see a humpback surface starboard, so close that a shower of seawater from its blowhole drenched her. Flinging water off her book, she grabbed the sides of the raft for support as the rubber tipped and shifted. Whale lovers screamed and trampled in her direction, tripping over each other to get the photo op. There wouldn't have been more chaos if the humpback had tried to mate with the boat.

She tried to scramble out of the way, but her bad

ankle got caught on a rope and she tripped before a portly man slammed into her. "Get . . . off . . . of me!" she managed. The man offered a vague apology before climbing to his feet and rushing to the latest sighting. Cameras whirred.

"Portside!"

Gripping the sides of the rubber raft, she gritted her teeth until the whale submerged and the crowd scrimmaged back to the front. She dropped back to the seat to examine her foot.

"Oh, yeah, that's gonna swell. Again!" she murmured, clamping her eyes shut.

Soaked pages in her novel curled in the sun.

Tess braked the rented car behind the hotel, exhausted. A trip to a local supermarket after whale watching for soda and chips to keep in the room proved interesting. Asparagus: nine dollars a pound. She didn't think she'd be cooking much asparagus if she lived here. She had purchased tape and an Ace bandage as well, since the first one smelled of seawater.

After dropping her goods in her room and

rebandaging her ankle, she made her way back out-side. The harbor gently beckoned to her. Lahaina was beautifully lit tonight. Festive strings of tiny multicolored lights reflected from boats tied to the moorings.

She walked slowly along the water's edge, drink-ing in the scenery. The air smelled tangy yet fresh. Palm trees rustled in the breeze. The ocean surf beat steadily along the shore.

Her eyes strayed to couples walking hand and hand, and emptiness welled inside her. Something was missing in her life—was it a man? Was it family? No, she didn't need a man to make her life complete, and her family had proven less than satisfying years ago. She didn't need anyone—maybe that was the problem.

Lanai Island lay dark against a background of sailboats awash in their tiny lights. A couple stood, arms wrapped around each another, and gazed at the splendid sight. She felt the weight of her aloneness. She *was* alone. Most of the time it didn't bother her, but seeing couples walking with their arms looped around each other, honeymooners kissing in secluded corners, made her realize what an empty life she lived.

Why couldn't she be like those people, tourists enjoying their vacation, laughing, enjoying life in general, even having their pictures taken with those ridiculous parrots in front of the hotel? She thought of the smiling tourists she'd seen crowded into shops, buying colorful Polynesian shirts and sarongs as if there would be a souvenir famine in the very near future. They'd never wear the things. They'd take them home, show them to their friends and families, and then they'd stash them in a bottom drawer and at some future time the treasures would go into a garage sale or become someone's Halloween costume.

Wasting money like it grew on trees—

She cringed when she realized how much like Mona she sounded. Mona.

The pit of her stomach felt like a stone. What difference did it make to her how those people spent their money? It made absolutely no difference to her. They were having a good time and that was what mattered, wasn't it?

Mona was the perennial wet blanket at every party, the one who couldn't have fun if her life depended on it: "Why would you buy me something like that?" she'd ask when Tess gave her a thoughtfully chosen birthday or Christmas gift. "What am I going to do with that? Such a waste of money."

Not much different than you wondering why tourists buy sarongs and brightly flowered shirts, is it, Tess?

Was she turning into her mother?

Sleep didn't come easily that night. Noises drifted

from the harbor—the sounds of happy voices, of someone strumming a ukulele and singing "Shiny Bubbles" and laughing.

People having fun. People unlike Tess Nelson, who'd die before she slaughtered the song, "Tiny Bubbles."

"Relax," she whispered. "Relax and enjoy Hawaii."

Connor.com *couldn't* run smoothly without her. Why, she'd established all of the H.R. systems, factors that kept the employees happy—everyone knew that happy employees equaled productive employees and that meant money in Connor.com's pocket. She was the backbone of the systems, which were the backbone of the company. Logic said Len needed her, that Connor.com needed her.

Logic.

Carter shoved his room keys into his pocket as he let himself into his room. He slid the window open to welcome a breeze and automatically turned on the TV. The cheeseburger he'd eaten fought with the double-dip Häagen-Dazs coconut pineapple cone he'd bought on the walk back to the hotel.

Sitting down in a chair, he propped his feet on the bed and adjusted the sound on the TV as his eyes scanned the stack of coupon books he'd acquired.

". . . tropical storm . . . better watch this one, folks, could be upgraded to hurricane status before the night's over . . ."

Spotting a coupon for "Mexican Madness Night" at Moose McGillicuddy's restaurant, he leaned over and carefully creased the paper, then tore it out. Two for $16.95. He shrugged. Not bad— he was a "one," but he'd eat what he could and leave the rest.

Adjacent to the Madness coupon was one for a free coffee mug with a twenty-five-dollar purchase at Hilo Hattie's. The binoculars and puka beads had already cost him fifty, but he might find something else he liked—maybe take Carl back one of those hula skirts. He snickered when he tried to imagine what the macho supervisor would do with two half coconut shells and a grass skirt. The coupon joined the others on the nightstand.

He stretched out to relax and let the cheeseburger settle. Carl had been smart to make him take a vacation. He'd needed the time away to refocus and relax.

Thanks for calling my limitations to my attention, he thought. *Help me to lean more fully on You.*

Clicking off the TV, Carter lay in the darkness,

doing what he'd come to do in Hawaii: spend time with his Best Friend.

Lord, You know my heart. Let me do more thanking and less complaining. Grant me patience to wait on You. I recognize my need for Your assurances, for Your strength, for Your hand on my life. I stand guilty: guilty of weak faith and the if-I-can't-fix-it-by-Friday-I'll-turn-it-over-to-God thinking. Thank You for reminding me that it is You I need, not You who needs me.

8

Startled from a sound sleep, Tess sat bolt upright in bed. Shouts—someone pounding on her door.

Fighting off the dregs of deep sleep, she shook her head and tried to focus on the lighted numbers on the travel alarm on the nightstand. Six a.m.? What was going on now? Deciding the racket wasn't going to stop, she grabbed her robe and stuffed her arms into it, then rammed her left foot in a loafer. Failing to find the other, she dropped to her knees to search under the chair.

Someone pounded on the door again, then a man's voice yelled out, "Open up!"

She found the missing shoe as the hammering persisted. Springing to her feet, she banged her lip on the edge of the bed frame.

"Ouch!" The tip of her tongue worried the swelling knot as she grabbed the shoe and stuffed it onto her right foot. "Ouch!" She'd forgotten the sore ankle. Fire alarms were shrilling in the hallway.

Her tongue was still exploring her bleeding lip as she reached the door and jerked it open to find a fireman in full gear standing in front of her, ax in hand, his face blackened with soot. Two air tanks were strapped to the man's back.

"What's going on?"

"We're evacuating the building."

She caught the scent of smoke. This wasn't a drill; it was the real thing. Panic swelled in her throat.

"We need you to leave the hotel immediately."

"Ah . . . yeah. I just need to—"

"Leave everything. Get out of the building." The fireman moved on.

"Take the stairs at the end of the hall. Don't use the elevator," the man turned to warn over his shoulder before he continued down the hall, pounding on doors and calling out evacuation orders. The firefighter's heavy black leather coat with Maui County Department of Fire Control disappeared into the blue haze hanging in the air.

Hotel guests in various stages of undress rushed past her. Coughing, she reached inside for her purse and then went to the bathroom to retrieve her glasses. As she passed room 215, the door flew open and Carter stumbled out.

"Are you still here?" Carter frowned.

"I had to go back for a minute."

"For what?"

"My glasses." Her mouth firmed. "I can't see without them and I didn't have time to put my contacts in."

Carter glanced at her door number. "What are the chances of us being on the same floor in the Mynah Nest and Pioneer Inn?" The siren kept up its blare as pajama-clad guests raced for the stairwell.

"Hey, you two! Keep moving. Get out of the building. *Now!*"

Carter grabbed her arm and propelled her toward the exit stairway. As he opened the heavy door, a cloud of thick smoke belched out, and he quickly shielded her with his body. Tess's mind raced as other people turned and searched for an alternate escape.

"Down here!" someone shouted.

She edged closer to Carter. "Do you have this uncanny feeling that we're caught in some ludicrous crisis time warp?" she said, trying to sound unconcerned even as tears stung her eyes.

"I'm beginning to get that feeling."

Her body trembled beneath her thin robe.

By now the firemen were swarming; one beefy man stood by a fire exit and motioned guests through an open window. Tess and Carter managed to keep ahead of the smoke. Fire sprinklers were going off; water ran along the carpeted hall in streams.

"Ouch!" she cried.

Carter stopped. "What?" He looked at her.

She pointed down. "My ankle." He scooped her up in his arms and raced toward the window, waiting until a man and his wife climbed out onto the metal stairway. Her fingers wrapped in his shirtfront. "I can't do this—"

"Sure you can—we're not talking options here."

She looked down at the thirty-foot drop, then back to him. "I can't do this. What if I fall?"

"You can do it." He gently pried her fingers loose from his T-shirt.

She shook her head, clamping her eyes shut tightly.

"Just hold on. I'll carry you down—"

"No! You can't!" Her grip tightened. "I can't—really. I can't."

"We're only two floors up. We'll be safe. I have eagle footing. Keep your eyes closed and pray."

"I don't pray . . ." she said weakly.

He glanced down, his face puckered in a frown. "Okay, I'll pray for both of us." He helped her through the window and climbed out. "Lord, we're coming through!" he shouted. Sirens wailed. Thick black smoke roiled from a downstairs vent. Firemen unraveled long water hoses from pumper trucks. Ladder trucks arrived.

She clung to his shirt, refusing to open her eyes.

"Just hold on." His voice was low, gentle. He started to ease his way down the fire escape. "We're going to make it just fine. Don't worry. Keep your eyes closed, and don't look down."

He cautiously felt for each step.

"Are you all right?" he asked.

"Are we down?"

"Not quite. Still one floor to go."

"Still one!"

"We're doing fine. Keep your eyes closed."

"Don't worry." It wasn't until he set her down on solid ground that she slowly loosened her grip. Fawn-colored eyes opened. She fumbled in her robe pocket and slipped on a pair of eyeglasses.

"You couldn't see anyway?" he exclaimed with a laugh.

"I wasn't taking any chances—all my clothes are up there. What about my clothes? I'm not dressed."

Carter ran his hand through his hair. "I don't know. We'll have to see how bad the fire is."

Someone handed the displaced guests cups of hot, fragrant coffee and a blanket, which Carter protectively wrapped around Tess. Threading their way through the crowd, they wandered across the street, sat on the curb, and stared at the ground floor where black smoke rolled from broken windows.

A moment later, Carter looked over to find a woman sitting on the curb beside him. Startled, he stared at the yellow cat draped around her neck in collarlike fashion.

The woman sent him a peripheral glance and smiled. "There's nothing like a bit of excitement to stir the blood, is there?"

"No, ma'am." His eyes focused on the animal. How did she get the cat to do that? Wasn't that thing hot around her neck? Where had she come from? He hadn't seen her at the hotel.

She gave him a smile peppered with experience. "Don't worry. God has everything under control."

"Indeed He does," Carter replied.

Nodding, he turned back to Tess, who leaned close and whispered, "I've seen her. She was sitting on the bench at the Banyon tree a couple mornings ago."

The lady turned with Tess's hushed observation. Their eyes met, and she smiled benignly. After a moment she turned back to stare at the historic old building engulfed in smoke.

"Everything we brought with us is up there," Tess said.

The woman nodded. "Clothing and luggage can be replaced. But a soul—now that's another thing. I must go, but I'll see you again." She stood and walked over to one of the waiting ambulances.

"She's an odd duck," Carter said more to himself than to Tess.

They watched as fire belched from the kitchen area and flames spread. He sat with his wrists hanging over his knees, staring at the ground. "This is turning into some vacation."

She laughed humorlessly. "And I came to Hawaii to get away from it all."

He smiled. "Me, too—I'm supposed to be relaxing. Too much stress in my life.

"Well—" leaning back on his elbows, he stared at the burning hotel, "things could be worse. Like the lady said, material possessions can be replaced. At least no lives were lost."

She nodded. "Wonder how the fire started?"

He shrugged, then sat up straighter. "I don't know about you, but I could use some breakfast. Are you hungry?"

"Well," she looked down at the robe and blanket, "I'm not exactly dressed—"

"Nobody's going to care. Let's find some scrambled

eggs. We're down to nothing except what's on our backs. Do you plan to starve, too?"

The corner of her mouth quirked. "No."

"Me either. Let's go."

He ushered her into the warmth of a nearby small café. The eating establishment was deserted—everyone, it seemed, was out watching the fire. Carter chose a table near the back of the room. She pulled the blanket closer around her robe as if it were a queen's cape, and sat with her back to the wall. Small tables with rush-bottomed chairs waited for customers. Vases of flowers placed on each table added a festive air, and a mural of palm trees and ocean waves covered one wall. The pretty waitress carrying menus and glasses of water looked as if she would feel right at home in a grass skirt.

"What can I get you?" the woman asked.

"Black coffee for me," Carter said without consulting a menu. "Two scrambled eggs, toast, and some of that tropical guava jelly."

Tess nodded. "Same."

The waitress smiled, a deep dimple creasing her twenty-something face. "You two from the hotel?"

"Yes."

"Too bad. Lose everything?"

Tess studied the table, the knuckles of her hand

white from clutching the blanket that wanted to slip off her shoulders.

"It would seem so," Carter answered. "I don't know when we'll know for certain."

"Lose your money, too?"

Carter had to smile. "I have my billfold."

"Well, if you need to run a tab—I'm Joanie, and I own the place."

"Thanks."

When Joanie left to retrieve their order, Tess planted her elbows on the table and thrust her fingers into her hair. "I simply cannot believe this!"

Carter shrugged. "Life sometimes throws sliders. The way I see it, we're still alive, we're in paradise, and this vacation has no where to go but up."

She leveled her gaze on him. "What planet did you say you were from?"

"Earth." He grinned, and then leaned closer. "Temporary journey until the real thing."

She groaned. "You're one of those Christians, aren't you? I knew when I saw you bow your head at the luau."

"You mean the fun luau? Yes," he said quietly. "I believe in God. He's seen me through a lot."

"I thought so. You're too . . . comfortable with disaster."

"I've never heard that one before."

"I'm sure you have your perfect little life; it's a free ride with God, right?"

"No." He leveled a gaze at her. "Why are you so uptight?"

That stopped her cold. She sat back and let her hands drop to the table. She looked down and noticed some stray strands of hair. Her face flushed.

"I'm not trying to offend you," Carter went on. "You just seem . . . stressed." She lifted her eyes to his.

"I'm not a Christian and I'm sorry I got defensive. Maybe I am stressed. With the fire and all . . ." Her gaze dropped to the bag in her lap. She laughed. "I just realized how stupid I am. I didn't grab my purse; I grabbed a makeup bag."

"Well, you may be broke but you'll look good," he said.

"I wasn't thinking," she said. "That's not like me. I'm usually a logical, organized, in-control person."

"Losing your britches to a fire will shake up anybody."

"It's *not* the fire—or Beeg being gone or the weather or losing my contact. It's *everything*—everything about this whole rotten episode called life."

The waitress set two cups of coffee on the table. Carter stared at the steaming liquid as silence took over. Finally he reached for sugar packets, eyeing her. "What do you mean by 'everything'?"

She sat silent for a moment, wondering if she'd said too much. Yet there was something about a man in a T-shirt and pajama bottoms and a woman wearing a robe and blanket that transformed strangers into confidants.

"I lost my job."

"Lost your job," he repeated. "That's all? I thought you were going to say you'd been given three weeks to live."

"I might as well."

"Come on, now. Losing a job isn't the end of the world. You're alive; you're in good health—I presume. You're in paradise." He smiled, as if hoping to coax the black look off her face. "What's so bad?"

"I was replaced by the boss's old fraternity brother. Fired."

Carter dumped sugar into his coffee. "That's bad."

She lifted an indifferent shoulder and grabbed for the blanket when it started to slide. "I know it probably sounds trivial to you."

"Well, no. Not trivial. But you have to admit it's not one for the books. It happens more than you'd think."

She absently shredded a napkin. "Dave—that was my boss's dad, who founded the company—had groomed me to be his right hand. I was in line to be the next vice president of human resources. I'd worked hard for the job—my private life the past five years has been practically nonexistent. But then Dave died suddenly . . ."

"And sonny came in and the dream disappeared."

"Pretty much. He did offer me another position . . ."

"And the choice was?"

"Payroll, two levels below my current position, or leave the company."

"Ouch."

She piled up the napkin pieces. "I think Len brought in his friend to get back at me. He seemed jealous of the working relationship I had with his father—he felt intimidated by me."

Carter sat back in the booth and studied her.

"That's pretty cold. Could be the best thing that's ever happened to you."

"Yeah, well, Len has quite an ego. I went back and realized I still had a plane ticket to Hawaii—it was supposed to be a business trip."

"He paid for this trip?"

"Well . . . technically . . . yes." She shifted in her chair. "It was a nonrefundable ticket . . ." her voice trailed off. She really hadn't given it much thought, but when put that way she felt a guilt she hadn't felt before. "I guess I should pay Connor.com for it when I get back . . ."

Carter smiled reassuringly at her. "So what are

you going to do for work when you return? A bright, intelligent woman like you shouldn't let one jerk get you down."

"Bright and intelligent, huh? I wonder what kind of impression you'd have of me when I'm not doing a Three-Stooge fest." She pointed to her ankle and puffy lips.

"It's in the eyes," Carter said, half joking.

"Oh, the eyes," she repeated. "Seriously, I don't know what I'm going to do. Yet." She balanced her coffee cup in one hand, studying the thick mug as if she'd never seen a cup before.

"So, now what?"

"Now I wait until Len realizes his mistake—and he will. He'll beg me to come back and I'll probably go—under my terms. I've spent too many years with the company to walk away now." She leaned back in the booth. "In another five years I'll move on, manage an even larger Human Resources department, and maybe even move into labor relations." She looked up sharply. "With my experience I can work anywhere I want."

He lifted his hands with mock surrender. "I'm on your side."

"Well, don't think for a minute that Len's decision is anything but a minor roadblock—because it isn't. I've spent the last five years building my career—Len

Connor isn't going to diminish it or *me* with one brief conversation."

"Got it all under control, do you?"

Joanie arrived with two plates and slid breakfast in front of Carter and Tess before pouring fresh coffee.

"Can I get you anything else?" Joanie asked.

"Nothing," Carter said. "Thanks."

The waitress walked off. Tess sat staring at the plate.

"Do you want something else?" Carter looked at her.

"I'm not hungry."

"You've got to eat something." Carter spread jelly on a piece of toast and held it out to her. "Try this. One bite at a time."

"I can't—"

"Tess Nelson's in control, isn't she? Eat."

She snatched the toast and bit into it.

"That's it—I love a woman with an appetite."

Picking up her fork, she sobered. She looked up, her eyes intent. "You talk to God, don't you?"

"Sure. My faith is important to me."

"I suppose He talks back to you?"

"Every day—in a loud, thunderous voice often accompanied by wind, thunder, and lightning." He took a sip of coffee, and then dipped his head when he saw the heat in her eyes.

"He doesn't *talk* to me—not in the way you imply. But we have ongoing communication."

She shrugged. "My grandmother took me to church once in a while, but I didn't then nor do I now understand all the hoopla. Lately I've been trying to comprehend . . ." She glanced out the front window of the café. "Right now I have more pressing concerns to consider; do I have any identification left, any clothes, and any money—"

"Don't worry about it. I'm sure the hotel will help."

She felt herself choke up—she wasn't sure why exactly, but she sure wasn't going to let Carter McConnell see her turn into a blubbering mass. "I thought about sending the tickets back to Len, but then I thought, why not? Why not get out of Denver, leave the snow and cold behind? That's easy enough, I thought. Consider my options.

"But then the taxi had no heater and I nearly froze. The driver drove like a maniac. I sprained my ankle at the airport and had to limp down the Jetway. When I got to Maui, a little boy ran into me, knocking my contact out. My best friend, whom I was really coming to see, is on the Mainland showing her watercolor originals." She sighed. "The luau was a disaster, the beach a worse failure, and now there's been a fire in the hotel kitchen, which happened to be directly below my room." She looked up. "Does this God of yours have a warped sense of humor?"

"Yes, God has a sense of humor, but it's not warped." He leaned closer and whispered lightly, "Nothing about God is warped. He loves us—without reservations."

Tess felt herself swallow hard. The kindness in his voice threatened her resolve to not cry. Carter straightened. "What about family? Mom? Dad? Brothers or sisters? Why not go home for a long overdue vacation?"

"Never. Mona wouldn't welcome the intrusion. She's the last person I want to know about losing my job. I haven't seen my brother in twenty years. He's off photographing another war somewhere—I can't remember the last time we talked."

"Mona?"

"My *mother.*"

The way she bit the word out translated to al-Qaida terrorist. Mona bin Laden.

His tone softened. "What a pair we make. I'm here in paradise because my boss thinks I'm stressed out; you're here because you *are* stressed out."

"I didn't say I was stressed out," she defended.

Carter smiled knowingly. "Okay. Never mind," she conceded.

She glanced down at her soot-blackened robe, the

blanket, and shrugged dismally. "I'm going home—
the moment the stores open and I can buy something
other than this robe and blanket to wear."

Carter salted his eggs. "I suppose—" His words
halted in midsentence as a man suddenly burst
through the restaurant's front door and barreled
toward the table. The Popeye—a spinach-eating
looking brute twice Carter's size and clearly of
Polynesian descent—grabbed him by the shirt collar
and pulled him out of the booth.

"What th—?" Carter's eyes bulged as the oaf dangled him in midair by the nape of his cotton/poly-
ester blend T-shirt. The hulk glared at Carter as if he
were about to take him apart piece by piece.

"The question is, what do you think *you're* doing,
chump!" The man's voice sounded like gravel on
metal.

"Let–go–of–me!" Carter wrapped his hands
around the man's tree-branch-like wrist and tried to
wrestle free. His air supply diminished.

Tess slid out of the booth, throwing down her
napkin. "You let him go this instant!" she demanded.
"Who do you think you are?"

Carter felt like a fool, dangling by his shirt collar
from the hand of this . . . this *leviathan,* while Tess
confronted the guy like a teacup poodle facing down
a pit bull.

She snapped her finger and pointed at the man with authority. "I'm warning you! *Let* go of him!"

Standing in bare feet, she was five foot nothing of blazing wrath in a nightgown and smoky bathrobe.

The bully let go of Carter's collar and shoved him against the booth. Carter felt his hip hit with a sickening thud. He straightened against the pain, about to pull himself up between Tess and the giant when Tess spoke again, her voice low but filled with grit, "Just what do you think you're doing?"

The man's cold eyes fixed on her. "This is between him and me, short stuff."

She got in his face. "Not when you come in here and disrupt my breakfast, buster!"

He started to ease off, shooting Carter a murderous glare. "I don't know who you are, lady, but this chump has been seein' my girl. Nobody cuts into my time."

"Wait a minute!" Carter protested, but Tess held up one hand to stop him.

"And who is your *girl?*" she asked coldly.

"Irihapeti Tehuia—ask him." He pointed at Carter.

"I not only don't *know* an Irihapeti Tehuia, I can't even spell it." Carter sat back down, raising a hand to his crushed windpipe.

"Never heard of her," the ape scoffed. "I got word

that you two was seen havin' a cozy dinner last Friday—"

"I wasn't in Hawaii last Friday." Carter met his furious gaze. "Your information is wrong."

"You—"

"He wasn't," she interrupted. "Neither one of us got here until Monday night."

"You'd lie for him—"

"Maybe. But I'm telling the truth right now." She crossed her arms, her eyes daring him to repeat his claim.

The brute's features coiled like a snake. "You're not Frank Lotus?"

"I'm not Frank Anybody. Look, fella, I don't know who you're looking for," Carter said, "but it isn't me. Why don't you just leave, talk to this woman you're having trouble with, and try to get the mistake straightened out." Carter massaged his swollen throat. The dufus had bruised his windpipe!

Pivoting on his heel, the stranger lumbered out of the café. Tess sank back into the booth and released a sigh of relief.

"Well, that was interesting," Carter said.

They sat for a moment, and then burst out laughing. Carter was glad to see that she was feeling better, even if it took his broken neck to wipe the gloom off her face.

"If this situation can get any worse, I'd like to know how," he admitted.

"Oh, I'm sure it can." She wiped her eyes with the corner of a napkin and eyed the mound of congealed eggs on her plate. "Actually, it's starting to get interesting."

9

"Alana has now been upgraded from a tropical storm to a hurricane. She could make landfall in the Hawaiian Islands within thirty-six hours. But she's switched course before. Stay tuned for updates as they become available."

The bartender reached up and switched off the news. Murmurs about the approaching storm spread among the guests, but Tess was oblivious to the gossip.

Sitting in the Pioneer Courtyard, surrounded by palms and lush vegetation, she and Carter waited for the hotel management's instructions on how to weather the storm.

With all the mishaps she'd had, the thought that she'd be smack dab in the center of a hurricane had never entered her mind.

She finished off a glass of iced tea and sat back. "You have been very nice about all this."

Carter had been more than nice; he'd been cour-
teous and kind and ever optimistic. That was more
than she could claim for herself.

Pioneer Inn management had rounded up the
fire-displaced guests and asked them to wait in the
courtyard for further instructions. A female employee
found a pair of jeans and a shirt for Tess, and she had
changed in the ladies' room. Carter and several other
men still wore pajamas. The smell of thick smoke
hung onerous in the air, and the guests buzzed with
stories of the harrowing escape.

"You've been a good sport, too," he acknowledged. "What did the doctor say about that ankle?"

Medical staff was on site to help, so she took the
opportunity to have the injury looked at again. By
now, a sprained ankle was the least of her worries.

"He said it's healing nicely."

"You're still limping."

"My ankle is the least of my problems. Where do
you think they'll put us now that the hotel is devas-
tated?" The first floor was a black pit, especially
where the kitchen had been. While the upper floors
had been saved from the fire's ravage they had not
been spared from the sprinkler system that had left
everything a soggy, dripping mess.

The hectic hours surrounding the kitchen fire
had shown people's true nature. Everyone was help-

ing the victims. The management provided free trays of food and fruit and hot coffee they brought from the nearby grocery. Strangers brought blankets, clothes, personal items. It was truly a heartwarming thing to see. The manager appeared. Tired lines around his eyes testified to the past tense hours. Clearing his throat, the short, pudgy man got the crowd's attention. "Best Western wants to assure each guest that they will be taken care of with the utmost expediency, and hotel management deeply appreciates each person's willingness to cooperate. We are trying to locate rooms for every guest, but it's proving to be a difficult goal. Hotels on the island are at their maximum because of conventions and the Skins games this coming weekend. At the moment, kind Lahaina residents are offering to take guests into their homes until other arrangements can be made."

Tess's gaze switched to Carter. "I don't want to stay with a stranger," she whispered. It was barely eight o'clock in the morning, yet she felt exhausted. She wanted to leave, to be back in her quiet, safe home. But, with the storm approaching, the odds of getting a flight back to the Mainland tonight were slim to impossible, though she certainly intended to try. If she couldn't get out, she was stuck. Stranded in paradise. The absurdity struck her as funny, and she supposed lack of sleep was the culprit more than true humor, because the situation was about as humorous as a bubble gum machine in a lockjaw ward.

Carter shook his head. "I don't like the thought either, but it sounds like we have little choice."

"We will have employees standing by to introduce you to your hosts," the manager went on. "In the meantime, coffee, tea, and breakfast rolls are being served."

Tess and Carter got up, milling with the crowd. Young men and women worked their way though the pack, taking names and addresses.

The manager waved to her and Carter as they stood to the side of the fountain. He approached, his ruddy features dark with concern. "Mr. McConnell and Miss Nelson—I am so sorry for this inconvenience. I have a lovely woman who is willing to open her home to you—"

Tess met Carter's gaze and shook her head.

"Miss Nelson doesn't feel comfortable staying with strangers," Carter said. "Is there someplace else we could stay?"

"Only the beach," the manager concluded, then shook his head. "And I wouldn't advise sleeping on the beach."

"No—of course not." Carter ran his hand over his whiskered jaw. "You mentioned a woman?"

"Stella DeMuer." He leaned in close. "Ms. DeMuer is a bit eccentric, but I can assure you she's perfectly harmless. She has a lovely beach home in Kihei with a guesthouse in back for your comfort, Mr. McConnell."

"Kihei—"

"Only twenty-five minutes from Lahaina—lovely town," the manager assured. "You have a car?"

"I have one," Tess said. "But I really don't like the idea of staying in someone's private home."

Carter spotted a woman walking his way, and he frowned when he saw the large yellow cat draped around her neck.

Tess paled and edged closer. "That's the woman we talked to after the fire, the one I met by the Banyon tree."

Stella DeMuer emerged, larger than life despite her petite size, her weather-beaten face wreathed in smiles. "Hello again. Please," she extended a blue-veined hand. "I have a very large house that I am too willing to share." She turned to look at the homeless throng and her features saddened. "Since meeting you this morning I am certain that you two are the ones I'm meant to help. Come." She extended a gnarled hand with rings on every finger to Tess. "A nice hot bath and a cup of Earl Grey will do you a world of good."

Tess backed up, eyeing the hand skeptically. She wouldn't rest a moment wondering what she'd gotten herself into. "If you'll excuse me, I need to make a phone call."

She slipped away, leaving Carter to deal with the woman. He shot her a questioning look, but Tess kept walking. If he wanted to take a chance that this DeMuer character might be an ax murderer, that was his prerogative. She was going to try the airport first.

The airline clerk only laughed when she requested a seat on the next flight out. "I have 198 seats and I've booked 207."

She bet the nine that showed up expecting to go home wouldn't see the humor.

"Monday night is the earliest I could manage—then you'll be standby. And with this storm coming, I'm not even sure about that . . . Unless you have the cash to charter your own flight. . . ."

Biting her lower lip, she switched to Plan X—the last option short of death, and punched the cell phone's automatic dial. The phone rang twice before her mother's familiar growling voice answered. "Yeah."

"Mona?"

"Tess?" She heard the expected sigh. "Now what's wrong?"

"I'm in a bit of a fix, Mother." She decided not to

sugarcoat the situation—it wouldn't matter to Mona anyway. She could be standing on the top of a high-rise with her hair on fire and Mona would only ask how much the call was costing. "I've lost my job. I'm in Hawaii, and the hotel where I was staying had a fire. I have no money, credit card, or identification." She swallowed, pushing back the bitter taste of gall obstructing her throat. "I need your help."

"Lost your job? What did you do now?"

"Nothing, Mona. Downsizing. It happens all the time." Lies, all lies, but the truth would matter less to Mona. Mother wouldn't care that she'd worked sixty- and seventy-hour weeks to please Conner.com, that she'd skipped lunches to stay on the phone with their health care provider while they ironed out their benefits package, that she'd searched the ends of the earth to find the best 401(k) for company employees. She'd endured crude jokes from VPs and fought off married men's advances—all without endangering the company/client relationship and all in the name of advancement. Yet Mona would see what she wanted to see.

Steel tinged her mother's tone. "A Nelson has never lost his job. Surely if you were attending to business the company would have found a way to keep you. How many times have I told you, Tess, you control what happens to you—don't be blaming your problems on downsizing. That's a tidy, predictable euphemism for being fired. Was it your stubborn pride? And what do you mean you're in Hawaii? Hawaii? How can you be in Hawaii if you've just lost your job? You bring about your own problems, exactly like Roy . . ."

Tess interrupted Mona's tirade. "Could you just *please* wire me five hundred dollars until I get back to Denver? I'll pay you back. Three days at most, Mona. I'm at your mercy."

There it was again. The sigh. The tedious, almost-silent I-wish-I'd-never-had-you sigh. Well, she wished the same thing, but neither she nor Mona could have do-overs.

"Do you think I'm made of money? I barely have enough to scrape by, thanks to Roy Nelson, your esteemed, drunken father. Do you think my mother thought about me when she kicked me out of the house at fifteen? I had nowhere to go, Tess. I had to depend on myself, and if I've taught you nothing else it's to depend on yourself. I'd do you no favor by pandering to your weakness. You were irresponsible enough to go to Hawaii without a job to come back to, now you figure a way to get back."

The line went dead. Tess closed her eyes, blinking back tears.

Fine. There went your Mother's Day card.

After setting the phone in its cradle, she rested her head against the back of her chair. Why had she called Mona when she knew what the response would be? Mona was as cold as penguin droppings. Especially since Dad had left her once the kids were grown. He died of liver cancer at the age of forty-seven.

Tess sucked in bitterly sharp air and huddled deeper into the lining of her thin coat as she followed Mona and Troy down the railroad tracks. Troy was only two years old. Tess felt that funny sickness in the pit of her stomach again, the one she felt every weekend. I hate weekends. I wish there were no such thing as Friday and Saturday. That was when Roy would stay late at the bars and come home with that awful smell on his breath. Then Mona would start yelling. If she'd only learn to shut her mouth when Dad told her to, things would be better. He wouldn't get so mad. He wouldn't hit her with a trowel of plaster.

Flecks of white dotted the back of Mona's print dress. Tess stared at the design as she walked. Today was Saturday. Saturday meant that he was drunk by noon; Saturday meant there would be no peace in the house until Sunday afternoon when he slept it off. Saturday meant they wouldn't go home until late. It was cold, so cold. Tess hated that. She hated the walking and sitting on the railroad tracks wishing she was anybody else on earth but herself. She thought about all the kids in school who were sitting in warm homes with kind, smiling moms and dads.

They sat down on the cold tracks. She wondered if a train would come by. Maybe it will hit us and kill us, she thought. Then Dad will be sorry.

She wanted to go home, even if Mona and Dad did argue. She hated this feeling.

"I'm going to leave him when you kids get bigger," Mona promised, glancing over at her.

She had heard that so many times that the promise didn't touch her anymore—it didn't make her happy or sad. It was just another promise from Mona, a promise not to be trusted.

"I *hate* this idea," Tess confessed as she drove the rental car down Highway 31. In the passenger seat, Carter frowned as he tried to decipher Stella DeMuer's directions.

"Ms. DeMuer is trustworthy or the manager wouldn't have set this up—and if I, for one moment, think otherwise we'll get out of there." The map rattled as he shook it out. "You have to admit that God's provided for us; we don't have to sleep on the beach tonight."

"Yeah, well, He could have done better—He could have gotten me on that flight home tonight."

"That would've been unfair to me. We're just getting to know each other." Carter grinned. "Relax. Before we know it—"

"What are we looking for?" Her voice . interrupted. "The directions say that once we pass Harlow's restaurant we keep going a few blocks. Apparently the DeMuer house faces the ocean, and the back of the house faces the highway."

She motored through the tropical streets of Kihei, past shops and restaurants, condominiums with vivid beds of draceana, heliconia, and anthrurium, coffee huts with signs touting lattes and piña colada smoothies. To Carter's left, senior tourists wearing khaki shorts, knee-high socks, and sandals took leisurely strolls, passed by an occasional jogger. Sun worshipers lay on the beach, determined to get as much benefit from the rays as possible, although the gentle breakers had been replaced by rolling whitecaps.

"Why do you think Stella wanted *us* as her houseguests?"

Carter refolded the map. "Maybe she's lonely and wants company."

"That's it over there." She pointed toward a house. "Number 204, right?" To the right, the beige stucco structure was surrounded by overgrown tropical vegetation. Baldwin pines jutted up beside the red-tile roof that reflected hot sun. The dwelling had been at one time a magnificent showcase of opulence and grandeur. But time and neglect had taken its toll. Today the house looked slightly run-down and sad.

Flipping on the turn signal, she turned into the driveway. Stella DeMuer was sitting on the back step, waiting to greet them. Her face lit with expectation as Carter got their smoky-smelling, damp bags out of the trunk and transported them to the back door.

"Welcome," Stella enthused, clasping her hands together theatrically. "I've been expecting you. Come." She got up, lifted her cat around her neck, and walked down the stairs, where she led Carter and Tess to a small guesthouse. She was wearing a funny-looking red hat and short veil, with a feather poking up.

"You should be comfortable here, Mr. McConnell. I had Fredrick lay out clean towels and soap for you." Tess lifted her brow, and Carter knew she was thinking the same thing: Fredrick? The old woman had servants—or was she living in the past?

"Please. Call me Carter."

"Of course, Carter. Such a handsome name."

The guesthouse was old but meticulously clean. A tropical-scented breeze filtered through partially opened vertical glass panes. Bookshelves lined two walls, and four matching watercolors, not prints, of surf and sand hung above the faded blue sofa. Oriental-style throw rugs were scattered over the tile floors. "Thank you. This is nice." Carter dropped his bags on the floor and looked around. "Very nice." He reached for a banana in the bowl of fruit "Fredrick" had left on the coffee table. "Tess and I appreciate your opening your home to us."

"Very kind of you," Tess murmured.

"Nonsense, you're doing an old woman a favor. I get very lonely here, and the days are very long. Now you, my dear Tess, will come with me." Stella turned and motioned to Carter. "You can come, too. I know you must be hungry."

She led the way back across the cobblestone drive and into a side porch. Glass stretched across the front of the house where sofas, settees, and overstuffed chairs, old but in their heyday pricey, were lined up in conversation nooks. Beyond the glass wall, the Pacific glistened as waves rolled in. Tess's bedroom sat off the kitchen at the back of the house. She laid down her bag, and Stella and Carter drifted off to make small talk and chicken salad sandwiches for lunch. She was grateful for some time alone and glad to get off her ankle.

She lay back on the sunshine-smelling pillowcase and closed her eyes. Maybe this wasn't such a horrible idea after all. She considered Carter's earlier remark about God being good to them. Indeed, they wouldn't have to sleep on the beach tonight, and Mrs. DeMuer seemed like a kind old lady, although she did find the cat thing more than odd.

She felt herself starting to drift as she listened to Carter's clear baritone drifting from the kitchen. Maybe, if she were a praying woman, she ought to thank God for pairing her up with this gentle man. He had helped her in so many ways with his kind yet no-nonsense approach to life.

She could have done a lot worse.

Later she sat in the kitchen and ate sandwiches and cheese curls with Carter and Stella. The cat occupied himself by taking a bath in the sunny alcove window. Perhaps things finally were turning around for her. She could only hope.

The earth softened around the edges; the sun slid lower, spreading an amber blanket across the water. Tess meandered down the beach alone. The wind was blowing hard now, tangling her long hair. Her gaze moved across the ocean. Heavy waves lapped the shore, and distant snapping sails sounded like mini-shotgun blasts.

What was she doing here on this beach? What was she doing in Hawaii when everything important to her was in Denver? This was insane. She should go home and get her life back on track. Mona was right; no one was going to wave a magic wand and make her troubles disappear. Certainly not Mona and certainly not Len Conner. She'd been foolish to ask for Mona's help. The woman had always been as cuddly as a porcupine.

Her greatest fear was that she would become Mona, that she would become a critical, joyless woman. Was that what she wanted? She despised the thought. She wasn't a child any longer. Mona was right about one thing—she needed to take charge, and the first area she was going to work on was not allowing Mona's nagging to keep sending her to that fearful place she'd gone to as a child. That cowering child with no self-esteem needed to be laid to rest. But that was easier said than done.

"Tess?"

She turned around to see Stella waving, the breeze battering her floral caftan. She waved back.

"Mind if I join you?" Stella said as she came closer.

"Come!" Tess said.

Stella walked with an amazing vitality for a woman her age. Tess guessed her host to be somewhere in her early eighties, but then she'd never been good at guessing ages.

She bit back a grin. At least this afternoon Stella had left the cat at home. The woman was warm, interesting, and definitely eccentric, yet Tess had never met anyone who intrigued her more.

"How is that ankle, dear? You haven't been walking too much, have you?" Stella's gaze was kind and very focused. She patted Tess's hand. "You look tired. Vacations are supposed to be restful."

The two women walked on. Stella lifted her face to the fading sun. "Trade winds have been higher than usual. Weatherman says there's a storm approaching."

"Thank you again for your hospitality," Tess said. "I won't be in your hair for long—I'm flying home Monday. Hopefully."

"So soon? Pity." She smiled at her. "The island is really lovely this time of the year. I'd be happy to show you the sights. You're welcome to stay with me as long as you want."

Her heart wasn't in it anymore. She'd been too beaten down.

"Thanks, but I couldn't intrude—"

"Intrude," Stella scoffed, waving a dismissive

hand. "I'm rattling around in that big house. All those rooms—for an old woman and a cat. Fredrick goes home at night. I love the company, and you're meant to be here. I know that with a certainty. You have things to learn, and I can help with that." Her eyes softened. They reached a sharp, rocky outcropping and turned back toward the house.

"Tell me about yourself," Tess nudged. "Have you always lived here?"

"Edgar had the house built in 1931. I waited until construction was complete before I moved here from Los Angeles." She smiled and her eyes crinkled as if her memories were sweet. Tess felt a tug of envy. Quite obviously Stella had loved this man deeply.

"Edgar? That's your husband?"

"Edgar's dead now, been gone over twenty years." Mist shimmered in Stella's eyes. "My, how I miss that old fella." She glanced over. "You and Carter are in love?"

"Me and Carter?" Tess choked out. "No—I barely know him. We met through a series of events, starting at the airport." As far as love . . . she wasn't sure she knew the meaning of the word. She'd been "in like" with men a few times. Respected one once, but love? She didn't know if she knew how to love.

"Stella, what made you decide to take us in? There are all kinds of sickos walking around. You don't know us—"

"I know you well enough." Stella smiled and nodded. "Yes, I know you well enough. It was meant that we meet."

Tess brushed a piece of hair out of her eyes and thought about Stella's declaration: *It was meant that we meet.*

What was that supposed to mean?

Friday morning, the aroma of hot coffee filled the air when Tess emerged from the bedroom. The previous night she'd managed to launder her smoke-laden clothes and air out her luggage. She'd gone to bed around 11:00 but rising wind had kept her awake most of the night. She smiled at Carter, who was stretched out across a lounge chair, reading a newspaper.

"Good morning," he said.

"Morning." Yawning, she scratched her hair and thought maybe she should have combed it into some semblance of order. She wondered if her bald patch was noticeable. She hadn't found any more hairs lately. Perhaps that malady was abating. She hoped. But then she wasn't trying to impress anyone. Her eyes moved surreptitiously to Carter, who didn't seem to notice the train wreck—or if he did, he was kind enough not to comment. Len would have said something.

Carter glanced up, his smile sending an odd shiver down her back.

Stella's lilting voice drifted from the kitchen. "Waffles and scrambled eggs coming up! Are you hungry?"

Not if you're cooking with a cat around your neck, Tess thought with a smile.

"Starved!" Carter said.

Tess wandered into the sunny kitchen where a large, open window carried the scent of fresh ocean air.

"Help yourself to the coffee, or there's fruit juice on the counter," Stella said in her sweet way. "Make yourself at home." She turned from the stove, clasping her hands. "I'm so glad to have someone to eat with this morning. This is wonderful."

"You're a godsend to us," Carter said as he walked into the kitchen. "Thank you, Stella." He stretched, then pressed his hand to the small of his back. "And my bad back thanks you. Just thinking about a night on the sand hurts."

Tess smiled. "Coward."

"When it comes to pain? You're looking at the worst." He winked.

Well, at least he was honest, she thought. Clean cut, nails neatly trimmed, hair cut in classic style, freshly shaven and smelling faintly of Old Spice, and *honest,* to boot—she'd begun to think the breed had disappeared with the T Rex.

"Oh, we'll have such fun," Stella crowed. "Now, you sit," she directed to Carter. "I'll take up the eggs." The waffle iron beeped that it was done. "Tess, would you work on waffles, please?"

Tess reached for a plate and the butter dish. "Sure."

"Here we go," Stella sang out softly a few minutes later, setting plates of steaming eggs and waffles in front of Tess and Carter, and then setting a third on the floor for the cat. "There now," she crooned, calling the cat from his spot by the window. "Eat up, Henry."

Henry. Tess glanced at Carter. The neck muff's name was *Henry.* She picked up her fork and was about to take a bite when she froze as Carter asked if he could say grace.

"Oh, would you?" Stella beamed.

Stella closed her eyes, hands clasped with reverence.

Carter bent his head and offered thanks: brief, but with such sincerity and sweetness of thought that Tess was afraid to look up. She'd never heard anyone speak to God like that before. It was as if God was his friend and not some distant deity who struck terror at will. When the amen sounded, she glanced up to see Carter unfolding his napkin, his eyes discreetly appreciating the mound of fluffy yellow.

He picked up his fork. "Food looks great, Stella."

Stella got up to pour herself a cup of coffee before rejoining them at the table.

"Aren't you going to eat something?" Tess asked Stella as she spread strawberry jam on a piece of toast.

"Oh, no." Stella waved a hand in the air in what was now a familiar gesture. "I'll eat later."

She felt uncomfortable with Stella watching, but she managed to devour the meal in nothing flat.

"So, you're going home Monday?" Stella asked.

Tess smiled. "I hope. I'm on standby. What about you, Carter?" She peered over the rim of her juice glass. "Are you going to try to get a flight out Monday?"

Carter resalted his food. "I don't think so—since I'm already here I thought I'd stick it out for a couple of weeks."

"Stick it out? That doesn't sound very vacationerish."

"The reason I'm here in the first place is to get rid of stress. I guess the Lord is holding me to my promise."

"The Lord does indeed hold us to our word." Stella propped her chin on her hands. "By the way, did you two know that pesky hurricane's turned directly toward the island?"

10

"You're going to get an ulcer from all of this." Carter sat on Stella's worn sofa, thumbing through a worn copy of the *New York Times* as Tess frantically dialed another number.

"I have to get out of *here*—did you hear what Stella said?"

Carter nodded. "A tropical storm has been upgraded to hurricane—but only an F-1 hurricane, Tess. It's just a gale. With the proper precautions we'll be fine."

"How do you know this?" She hadn't allowed a forecast to register since leaving Denver.

"I'm an air traffic controller at O'Hare. I know my storms."

The man was the Rock of Gibraltar. Didn't he know that he and his "flight controller's" attitude were about to be blown off the face of the map?

She dialed the third charter flight number and met with the same results: no flights were leaving the island until the storm passed. Slamming the receiver back into the cradle, she dropped into a chair and crossed her arms.

"Need a Tagamet?" Carter said, his gaze never leaving the magazine.

"Very funny." She turned to him. "Aren't you the least concerned that we're *trapped?*"

"I'm concerned, but I'm smart enough to know that I'm not in charge of the situation." He got up to look out of the windows. Wind lashed the tops of palms; a garbage can lid whipped by the window. "I called to find out where the nearest shelter is—if we need to go there we can."

"We'll be safe," Stella said. She sat on the sofa with the cat around her neck again, a pleasant demeanor on her face. The cat appeared to be sleeping placidly. "Henry and I have ridden out many a tropical storm and lived to tell about them. Remember '92, Henry? Hurricane Iniki. It was September; the storm wasn't predicted to have any effect on the island, but we woke to the sound of air-raid sirens. Iniki had decided to do a switch-back overnight and was headed straight for us. I filled every pot and pan in the house with water—even filled the bathtubs. The radio said to put plywood on all the windows. I watched television until the announcer said the power would be turned off when the wind speed reached 45 knots, and that we should expect sustained winds to 165 miles per hour. Iniki had become a category five hurricane—the largest they get." Stella reached up and ran a spider-veined hand along Henry's side. "We did our share of visiting with the Lord that night, didn't we, boy?"

Tess got up and began pacing.

"Relax," Carter advised. "We'll take whatever precautions are needed." He glanced at Stella. "Do I need to do anything? Nail plywood, close the storm shutters?"

Stella smiled. "Not yet. Let's see what Ms. Alana does next. Often storms veer off and we just get the rain and wind."

Tess closed her eyes and rubbed her temples. She felt a pressure in her head that she was certain would balloon into an aneurysm any moment. Why weren't they doing *something*? Surely there was some precaution they could be taking other than this maddening sitting and waiting around for whatever came their way. This just wasn't right!

Seconds later, she felt the gentle pressure of Carter's hand on her right shoulder. She opened her eyes. "The NHC has issued a 'Hurricane

Watch'; this means the storm will make landfall normally within twenty-four hours—but the watch usually includes a fairly wide area. It's late in the year for hurricanes. Like Stella says, could be we'll only get gale-force winds, high water, and flash flood situations."

"And this doesn't alarm you?" Where *was* the Tylenol?

"All flights will be canceled until the storm abates," Carter said, a sympathetic look on his face.

"Come sit, dear." Stella patted the seat next to her. "We'll likely have a rough time of it, but nothing our Lord isn't in charge of. We'll be fine."

"The point is," Carter added quietly, "we need to heed the warning and take precautions. But we're here, Tess, under God's grace and His protection."

Grace. God had never shown her any grace. Had He shown grace by letting Len fire her? Had He shown grace through Mona? Had He shown grace by putting her in a situation in which she had no control?

"How long does it take for a hurricane to pass?" she asked weakly.

"The storm will be here in a few hours, most likely, and then runs its course in ten days or less," Stella said.

Ten days.
And Tess couldn't do a thing to stop it.
Grace.
She might as well wish for a million dollars.

11

Mid-afternoon, rain began as a faint pitter-patter, nothing to hint at the hulking monster it was destined to become. But soon heavy wind gusts battered the beach house's windowpanes. Tess sat listening to the storm's growing fury.

After a while she got up to pace. Peering outside, she turned around to face Carter, who was listening to radio reports on the storm. "Shouldn't we close the shutters?"

Carter looked to Stella.

She nodded. "You may close the shutters—but we'll wait another hour or two before the plywood goes up. I keep enough in the garage for just such an event."

"What about moving to higher ground?" Tess thought about Kula—the town was high atop Maui.

"Absolutely not!" Stella's chin shot up. "I will not

leave my home. We'll wait—see if it's upgraded. I've been through many a warning—some legitimate, some a waste of time and money. We'll wait." She absently stroked the purring cat's neck.

Tess could not understand Stella's ability to just sit there. Neither Stella nor Carter seemed worried, although she had detected a faint light of concern in Carter's eyes now that the wind had picked up. She wondered if Stella was truly of sound mind or if she and Carter should overrule her wishes and proceed with defensive measures. She looked over at Carter who said, "I'm going to check out that garage—see how well stocked we are. Just in case." His gaze shifted to Stella. Tess breathed a quiet sigh of relief— at least someone was moving forward.

"Do you need some help?" she whispered.

"No," he said. "You keep an eye on our hostess. I'll see to things." He quickly left, and she returned to her stool by the counter.

"So, Stella," she said. "What did you and Edgar do before you moved to Hawaii?"

"Oh, we lived in Beverly Hills. That's where all the movie people lived. Guess perhaps they still do—." Her voice drifted off.

"Were you and your husband in the film business?"

Stella laughed. "Oh, yes, I was but you wouldn't remember. You're far too young. And they don't show my movies on the late, late, or even very late show anymore." She chuckled.

Tess turned. "You were a movie star?"

"Oh my, yes. Starred with some of the biggest. Why I—have you seen *Orphans of the Storm*? No," she mused, "I supposed you wouldn't have—that was 1922."

1922? That made her what—over one hundred years old? Tess was amazed at the woman's memory.

"What about *Three on a Match*? No, I made that film in 1924."

"You were a silent film star?" Stella DeMuer suddenly fell into place in Tess's mind. She could picture eccentric Stella in the old melodramatic films with heart-tugging plots.

Stella's bottom lip quivered. "Surely you've seen *Casablanca*?"

Tess grinned. "You were in *Casablanca*? With Bogart and Bergman?"

"Oh yes—and that lovely Paul Henreid. Paul was such a gentleman, you know. Of course, that was later, when speaking parts were in—and truthfully, I had a supporting role in that particular film. Edgar, my husband, was unhappy about the casting, but I seized the opportunity to work with Humphrey and Ingrid," she confessed.

Humphrey and Ingrid.

"Then of course there was *Anna Christie,* with Greta—"

"Garbo?"

Stella blinked. "Why, yes—is there another Greta?"

"No—there isn't another Greta Garbo." Tess chuckled.

"*The Girl from New York* was my favorite, but then there was *Moonbeam, Jacob and Esau*—I played their conniving mother. I loved the part. Oh, there were a dozen others, names only those interested in movie history would recognize today."

"Why, you were a movie queen!" Tess said, amazed. She moved to the couch next to Stella and pulled a pillow onto her lap as she drew her feet underneath her. The wind beat against the panes. "I've seen *The Girl from New York.* It's timeless. Was your husband an actor as well?"

Stella blushed at the question. "He was a director in the mid- to late forties. We met on the set of *Moonbeam.* I was just twenty and he was twenty-five. I remember . . ." She paused and looked over at Tess with a faraway gaze in her eyes. "He was talking to the cameraman and, well, there was just something in his eyes. I can't really explain it. He was such a good man. It wasn't long before we were very much in love."

Tess felt a second twinge of envy. The love shimmering in Stella's eyes when she spoke of her husband, even after so many years, was real. Magic.

"We were married twenty years when he died." Her features closed momentarily. "I still miss him so much sometimes it's a physical ache." She dipped her head and blushed and the smile returned.

"I don't know if I'll ever find a love like that," Tess confessed.

"You have to start with trust—if you don't have that you don't have anything."

"I haven't been too successful in that arena—"

Carter came back. Water dripped off his rain slicker. "It's wet out there."

Stella pushed out of her seat. "Well, now, it's getting to be our nap time. You two just make yourselves at home. We'll keep a close eye on the storm." She picked up Henry. "Come, my love. It's nappies for us."

When the former movie queen reached the doorway, she suddenly turned. Her eyes softened. "Don't be afraid of life, Tess. Put your trust in Someone who deserves it. God is good; He keeps His promises when no other will." She turned and disappeared down the long hallway.

Tess gazed at the spot where she had stood. *Put your trust in Someone who deserves it?* For some unknown reason, she wanted to do just that—she wanted to trust, to find someone worthy of trust.

For a moment neither she nor Carter spoke. Then she said cautiously, "Do I look like someone who can't trust? What's with that remark?"

Carter lifted an innocent brow. "A nap doesn't sound like a bad idea."

12

"The NHC has now upgraded Alana to a category two storm." The TV meteorologist waved his hand over the mass of white on the map behind him as he spoke. Carter sat watching, a warm cup of coffee in hand. "The eye of this dangerous storm is expected to make landfall in the early hours of Saturday morning, the 24th on the island of Oahu. Island residents should be making plans to move to nearby evacuation centers. Remember to take your Disaster Supply Kit. Do not forget to make plans for pets if you must evacuate. Alana is a treacherous category two hurricane with winds capable of 96–110 miles per hour."

Carter switched off the TV and clasped his hands together across his knees. Sheets of heavy rain pelted the windows. He needed to find a way to protect Tess and Stella, even if Stella refused to move to the storm shelter. He reached to pick up his Bible, looking for the true Source of wisdom he'd learned to rely on. Tess thought he wasn't scared. Right. With a hurricane forming outside their window.

Lord, if only I were spiritually mature enough to trust You totally in the face of danger. I ask Your shield for Tess and Stella. Grant me the wisdom to do all that I can to protect these two women.

Could he help Tess? She needed more than shelter in a hurricane; she needed protection from a danger far greater, one all men were powerless against without God's help. Yet she seemed unwilling to relinquish that control to anyone but herself. Was he "man" enough to step out of his comfort zone and offer a solution—with God's Word to back it up? Face-to-face witnessing never came easy for him. He'd learned long ago that he couldn't whip a person into submission; the need and desire had to be there to begin with.

Instead, his witness was to build houses for orphaned children and tell them stories about God's love, but the innocent eyes that had looked back at him then were childlike, trusting. Experience had hardened Tess's eyes. Someone somewhere had instilled doubt in her, and he would bet the problem went back to an early age. It troubled him to see a young woman wrestling with life when relief was near and so obtainable. She had such potential, far beyond what she could accomplish at a job.

Carter thought back on his own journey toward God. He had accepted the Lord as Savior after a chain of rebellious years. He'd hit bottom, and he'd hit hard—social drugs, drinking, and wild women. He'd thought life couldn't get any better until he looked in the mirror one day and saw an empty shell of a man. He'd been missing work, losing friends. His life had become a cesspool so dank that he didn't know how to climb his way out. That was when a next-door neighbor had invited him to attend a men's retreat.

At first Carter had laughed. Men's retreat. At the time the event held the same attraction as a Barbie Doll convention.

But for some reason he'd gone. Life had gotten so unbearable, he knew his next step would've been suicide. That weekend he'd ended his restless search. He'd found what every man, woman, and child wanted: significance, security, and acceptance.

Could he share his faith with Tess? How would she react? Would she think he was a religious fanatic—a kook?

He suspected she already did by the looks she gave him when he prayed or picked up his Bible.

Am I not still God? a voice whispered.

Resting his head on the chair back, he closed his eyes and communed with the still, small voice, ever present.

When he opened his eyes, wind still battered the shutters and tore at the canvas awnings as though they were made of paper. Even with the storm upgrade, Stella had made it clear that she would not leave her home. The beach was the worst place they could sit it out, but Carter didn't intend to leave the old woman alone. He consoled himself that if the house had withstood a category five hurricane then surely it would hold tight in this storm.

The door suddenly flew open and a frenetic Tess appeared in the front hallway. Carter bolted, feet flying upward. Muddy water pooled on her tennis shoes. Her hair was plastered in wet, noodlelike strings to her head. Slamming his hand to his heart, he asked above the thrashing jackhammer of the wind. "What happened to you?"

"I was out on the lanai—this thing is getting worse." She pointed to the sheets of water running down the window glass. "We've got to do something."

Closing his Bible, Carter laid it on the table. "Stella isn't going to leave, and I'm not leaving her here alone."

"Six-foot breakers are battering the shoreline. It won't be long until the roads are impassible." She brushed past him to approach the window. "I'm scared, Carter. Honestly scared. We could be killed in this thing."

"We could get killed crossing the street." Taking her by the arm, he gently drew her away from the frightening sight. "Is Stella awake?"

"I don't know—I don't think so."

Stella walked into the room, blinking sleep from her eyes. "My, it's nasty out there, isn't it?" she said with her gaze toward the window.

The former movie star was wearing Henry. The cat snoozed, perfectly at ease with Nature's show of fury.

Carter frowned. "Stella, the storm has been upgraded to an F-2 hurricane. We need to do what we can to save the house, and then get to a public shelter."

"No," Stella contended. "I told you I won't leave my house." She smiled. "It's like an old friend; I need to be here to protect it."

Carter wheeled Stella's old '72 Chevy pickup around the barricade and headed back on 36. "Stella has plenty of plywood and nails for the windows—if it isn't too windy to put them up now. Thank heavens her house is only one story," he said. "There's an old generator too, but I don't know if it works—it looked awfully old. We'll pick up fresh flashlights and radio batteries and buy an emergency kit—canned goods, that kind of thing. Then we need to find out where we need to go when this thing *really* hits."

Tess looked out the windshield at the slanting rain. "*If* we can go anywhere."

He grimaced. "You're right. There's nowhere to run but into the ocean."

She swallowed back her rising panic as the truck plowed through sheets of standing water.

Wal-Mart was teeming with frantic islanders preparing for destruction. They ran toward the entrance with their hoods and purses held over their heads as if that would keep the pummeling rain from reaching them. Carter parked the Chevy on the last row adjacent to the blue-and-white building and they made a run for the front door.

Once inside, Tess headed for batteries while Carter wandered off in the direction of the snack bar. Tess hurriedly gathered a handful of C, AA, and D batteries, then proceeded to a long line where she waited for over half an hour to make the purchase. Her feet hurt, and her hair looked like a wet dog's fur. She'd give a king's ransom for dry underwear.

She heard snatches of anxious inquiries.

"Is the storm still moving in our direction?"

"Has it picked up speed or strength?"

She gazed along the rows of shoppers and saw Carter rolling a cart loaded with a small portable generator and black, heavy plastic sheets. Among the storm paraphernalia, he'd set a tuberose lei. He held two cups of steaming coffee in his hands. Handing one to Tess, he then draped the floral offering around her neck with a smile. "I thought you could use a pick-me-up."

Touched by his simple act of kindness, she nodded her head and gratefully accepted the hot coffee— how he'd managed to roll a cart and carry two steaming cups without losing the contents confounded her.

Men.

Carter was pounding on the defroster when she climbed back in the truck cab. He'd thoughtfully pulled to the front entrance so she wouldn't get wetter. "It's not blowing right," he explained before starting off again. Wheeling back onto the highway, Carter eased to the edge of the seat and mopped up moisture coating the inside of the windshield. The old heater clanked and chugged, and worn wipers tried in vain to keep up with the steady downpour.

"I read an Oprah book once about a woman whose boyfriend dumped her off at Wal-Mart and never came back." She held the dashboard with a white-fingered grip as the rain slanted in its heavy beat. Sweat beaded on her forehead.

"Really?" Carter reached over her to mop the passenger side of the windshield.

"The woman lived there for a few days without anyone noticing."

"Lived in Wal-Mart?" Carter said as if it were a sunny day and they weren't driving through foot-deep flooded streets.

"Yes—and she was expecting the moron's baby. Had the child on the pots and pan aisle—or somewhere like that, if I'm remembering correctly. The employees found her the next morning. That must have been pretty shocking." She lifted one hand to wipe her forehead and ran her fingers through her hair. Five or six hairs came loose in her hand. She looked out the window.

"You can see the road okay?" She asked, wondering if she would be able to find the pavement in these blasts of wind and rain.

"We're fine." He put a hand consolingly on her arm. "You can calm down."

Sheathed in the cab's rain-tinged air, she started to relax. She edged closer to him, hanging on to his sleeve. He turned to look at her and grinned. Shame washed over her. He had to deal not only with a hurricane but with a hysterical woman. She'd bet his challenges at O'Hare paled in comparison to this. Yet she'd never heard him complain.

She eased closer to his warmth and ignored the curious look he gave her. Their closeness allotted a sense of security—as if he had a direct pipeline to . . . well, somewhere . . . or someone that she didn't. She supposed some men would consider the move a come-on, but Tess wasn't thinking about propriety. She just wanted to feel safe. Sitting near like this, breathing in his cologne mingled with the tuberose of her lei . . .

Well, a woman had to admit that his thoughtful gifts were special—nothing like the obligatory red roses or Godiva chocolates that made a woman shun the scales for weeks afterward.

Carter McConnell was a nice guy—and the only thing solid she had to hold on to right now.

"I admire your composure," she admitted as Carter drove the pickup through the streets.

He chuckled—a nice, manly baritone timbre that gave her tingles. *Tingles. Whoa, Tess.*

"On the inside, I'm just as scared as you are.

Maybe even more," he admitted. "I have yours and Stella's safety to consider."

A man willing to admit weaknesses.

"But you don't show it—you seem so . . . calm."

"If I am, the credit belongs to the Lord, not to me."

She averted her gaze to stare out the window.

They fell silent as he wiped the windshield clear again.

"You think I'm terrible, don't you?"

He crammed the rag in his side pocket. "No. Why would I think you're terrible?"

"Because I don't *believe.*"

"Faith is an act of the will; you have to desire to know the truth, and you haven't desired it yet."

"And what is that supposed to mean?" Even as the words left her lips, she realized she sounded defensive.

"If I tell, you will think I'm a religious fanatic," he said.

"Too late; I already do." She grinned, then sobered. She'd seen him pray before every meal, read his Bible, saw him live as if his faith were something alive and real. Hardly the stuffy religion she'd heard about from Mona.

"Okay," Carter said. "You asked."

"I asked."

His eyes softened, and he spoke calmly without

censure. What she heard in his voice was concern for her, love. "No one can believe without the Spirit's help."

"Then you're saying God picks and chooses who will know Him? That hardly seems fair."

"God opens the doors, invites us to come to Him—He loves everyone, Tess, including you. But He's like us; He doesn't stay where He isn't wanted." Carter glanced over to meet her eyes.

Why, he *was* a religious nut, trying to frighten her into believing! She looked away. "Sorry. I can't understand the concept of a loving God. Sometimes I think He's downright mean."

"He is a God of justice and a God of mercy."

"Mercy. Now there's a crock. Where was God on September 11, 2001? Where was God when my friend Jennifer's husband died of brain cancer and left her with two young daughters to raise?" she asked.

Where was God the day Mona Nelson gave birth to her? She glanced at Carter as tears glistened in her eyes.

Carter reached over and rested his hand on top of hers. "I can't explain the bad things that happen in the world; I don't even try. But I do know that without the Holy Spirit a person is incapable of grasping God's words, and without God, life is meaningless.

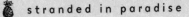

Acceptance is an option. But for me God's love was so compelling I couldn't resist it. It's the only thing that gives me hope in this world."

She turned her head to gaze at the pouring rain as his words resonated strongly within her. Right now, hope was what she desperately needed.

13

"Hurricane. From the Taino word meaning 'evil spirit.' In the Caribbean the storms are called the 'God of All Evil,'" Stella said as she sipped hot cocoa.

Carter had gone out to the garage to get the plywood to begin boarding the windows.

Tess divided her attention between the kindly old woman and another television weather bulletin. She turned her head to scrutinize the strengthening storm out Stella's front windows. The monster was getting down to business. Palm trees bent their heads to the bully, deferring to its greatness.

"Beautiful, isn't it?" The featherlike touch of Stella's hand on her shoulder drew Tess from her reverie. Breakers lashed against the fawn-colored sand, churning it to dark chocolate, kicking up heavy spray. An *a lae keokeo*—Hawaiian coot—drifted with drafts, his shrill cries echoing through the stormy late afternoon.

"Even in her fury, Nature is an awesome sight." Stella spoke in a soothing, confident tone—one Tess knew should have calmed her. Her thoughts kept returning to Carter's words on the way home from Wal-Mart: *It's the only thing that gives me hope.* The thought had begun to take root in her heart, and now it seemed to echo over and over, answering her heart's plea.

"I never cease to be amazed at His power." Stella's voice interrupted her reverie.

"God's power?" Tess tasted the name on her tongue, foreign—neither sweet nor sour.

"God's power. If you'll excuse me." Stella tuned and left her alone in the living room. Rain lashed the window.

Tess closed her eyes and drank in the scent of the rain. Her thoughts drifted. What kind of man was Carter McConnell? Certainly the first man she'd ever met who openly spoke of his faith, of commitment to God. She wasn't sure what to think about that. Her grandmother's faith was born of the need to avoid hellfire rather than the alive kind of faith that Carter claimed.

She had always felt that Christians made awkward, bumbling attempts to express *why* they were so happy, why they existed in a perpetual state of spiritual euphoria. Carter had experienced no such hesitancy. He truly believed what he practiced.

She turned from the window as Stella breezed back through the doorway, carrying a large tray filled with a teapot and two cups. A plate of lemon cookies sat beside the cream and sugar.

"Thought you might enjoy something warm. I wonder how Carter is managing that plywood."

Tess turned on the threadbare sofa and leaned forward to accept her tea. "I should go help him." Her thoughts returned to their current dilemma. The storm's intensity grew minute by minute. Outside, torrential rain hammered the storm-tossed sea, scattering sea foam like dried orchid petals. She felt a sudden urgency to go help Carter even though he'd told her he wanted her to stay with Stella.

"It should have been done earlier," Stella confessed. "Fredrick's talked about it for days, but you never know about these storms. Often they blow themselves out before they hit land. Who would have thought that with the normal threats behind us a rebel cyclone would decide to rear its ugly head in January?" She lifted the cookie plate to offer one to Tess before placing it back on the coffee table. "Would you do the honors, dear?"

Shutters banged against the stucco exterior.

Stella frowned. "I do worry about Carter out there. I wonder if he'd like some tea. It's chamomile."

Stella glanced over and her tone softened, "He'll be fine, dear. If he needs your help he'll tell you."

Startled that her thoughts had been so easily read, Tess changed the subject. "You said your husband was a movie director?" She noticed with a frown that the spoon was tarnished yellow. She wondered if Stella would mind her polishing the silver; she was still itchy to help in some way—*any* way.

"Yes—but I doubt you'd know any of his films." Stella proceeded to name half a dozen films that Tess had indeed seen on the Nostalgia Channel. After telling her so, Tess grinned and spooned sugar into her cup. "I'm honored to be in the company of a *famous* Hollywood celebrity."

"Well, you shouldn't be." Stella laughed ruefully. "Scandalous would be a better word choice."

"Oh?" Her smile faded.

"My husband was called to appear before the Army-McCarthy hearings."

Tess slowly lowered the cup back to the saucer. McCarthy hearings. Didn't that have something to do with a Hollywood blacklist back in the fifties? "I've heard of the hearings; I'm not sure what they were about."

"They were nothing but a witch hunt," Stella snapped. The old woman visibly bristled, her eyes turning as chilly as the howling wind. "The hearings were convened to investigate a series of charges leveled by Senator Joseph McCarthy."

"By the army? How did your husband get involved?"

The old woman's eyes hardened. "It's a complicated story, one much too involved to tell."

"No." Tess scooted to the edge of the sofa. "Please. I'm interested."

For a moment it looked as through Stella wouldn't comply—that the memory was still an open wound. Then, slowly, she set her cup back on the tray. The thin china rattled. "It was Edgar's destruction."

Stella studied her cup for a moment, and then continued, "McCarthy had a consultant on his staff named David Schine who was drafted into the army in 1953. Roy Cohn, McCarthy's chief counsel, began a personal campaign to pressure military officials into releasing Schine from service, though he'd been drafted, so he could return to Washington. Early in 1954—March, I think—the army retaliated by documenting what they called Cohn's 'improper intrusions' into Schine's military career. McCarthy responded by claiming the army was holding Schine 'hostage' to keep his committee from exposing communists within the military.

"Well, it rolled on from there. The Senate Permanent Subcommittee on Investigation, of which

McCarthy was chairman, voted to investigate. They also decided to allow live TV coverage of the inquiry." Stella glanced up.

"You weren't born yet, of course. For four years, beginning in 1947, McCarthy had been accusing people of being communists, destroying the lives and careers of ordinary people, and a number of people in the motion picture industry, but no concrete evidence had ever been shown that linked any of the accused to the Communist Party. But that didn't stop him.

"Several hundred performers whose only 'crime' was belonging to or supporting organizations or causes that McCarthy named as 'subversive' were blacklisted. No one would hire them."

"Couldn't someone do something?" Tess asked. "I mean—"

"The Screen Actors Guild, the Screen Writer's Guild, the Screen Directors Guild made no effort to stop this . . . this evil. On the contrary, they cooperated. If they tried to protect their members, they knew that the American public would think the guilds themselves were subversive, which would mean the public would stop going to movies, which would lead to a massive loss of jobs.

"One accusation was that the communists were placing subversive messages into Hollywood films and were in a position to put negative images of the

United States in films that would have an international distribution."

Tess leaned back to digest the information. "And your husband was involved?"

"Yes, Edgar was involved. In 1946 the Screen Actors Guild was listed as a union with communist influences. So, some so-called friendly witnesses were called before the Un-American Activities Committee to be interviewed. Robert Taylor, Richard Arlen, Adolphe Menjou. Jack Warner, head of Warner Brothers Studio, named people on the studio's payroll that he suspected of harboring left-wing sympathies, including my husband."

"*Was* he involved?" she asked.

Stella drew a deep shuddering breath, and Tess could see that simply talking about that time in her life disturbed her. "I'm sorry. This is too sad for you."

The old woman stroked Henry, her eyes misting with unshed tears. "It's still painful, yet when I look back on my life I see this as one of those defining moments on which life-altering decisions were made. Edgar was called before the committee in Washington, D.C. He didn't want me to come, and I was busy on a film so I didn't go. Now I wish that I had. I'd have known what was happening. He never talked about it later, but I knew Marsha Hunt and she told me what happened.

"Marsha, too, had been blacklisted. She went to Washington with Humphrey Bogart, Lauren Bacall, and Danny Kaye. They hoped to generate positive publicity for those trying to defend themselves against those horrible charges, but their good intentions backfired. They had prepared statements that they planned to read when called to witness. But only one was allowed to read his statement. The rest were dismissed from the witness table, almost before they started.

"Anyway, others had better luck. Lucille Ball's testimony was so garbled and meaningless that she was allowed to be excused without stigma. That wasn't like Lucy at all—Lucille was a brilliant woman. If only Desi could have stayed away from the women . . .

"Writers like Clifford Odets never wrote again. Others managed to work behind the scenes, using other names, or worked in Mexico and in Europe. The rumor mill said John Garfield's death was linked to his appearance before the committee. It was an awful time." Stella shook her head as if to clear away the memory.

"Many directors kept working but changed their names. Edgar wouldn't do that. He said he couldn't pretend to be someone or something other than what he was. He was called before the committee after being named by Jack Warner; we don't know how that happened. Jack was probably trying to protect his studio. We could never find any real reason for his actions."

"It must have been a terrible time for both you and your husband." Tess stared at the cold cup of tea.

"Edgar never worked again." Stella's trembling fingers wrapped around her coffee cup. "He told the committee that he'd never been to any kind of meeting that could be called communist. I wasn't sure. I wasn't sure what was right or wrong, truth or lie. People you trusted turned on friends. You didn't know if you were next. It was a horrible time.

"Edgar went into a depression. Nothing I could do or say would draw him out of it."

"You . . . had reservations about your husband's innocence?"

Stella's head snapped up. "I'm sorry to say that I did—at first. There were days, sometimes weeks, when I was confused. Edgar refused to deny or confess anything. He was a man of principle," she said proudly, "and he expected his actions to speak louder than any statement. We left Hollywood and moved here, to Maui."

"Was your husband's name ever cleared?"

"Eventually, but it was too late. By then he was dead."

Tess cleared her throat to break the rickety silence. "I'm so sorry. It's so unfair."

Stella looked up, her hands resting on Henry's glossy coat. "Life isn't about fairness."

Tess kept silent.

"I should have trusted Edgar more; I wouldn't have missed out on one of the most important things in my life: the ability to help Edgar in his darkest hour." Her eyes met Tess's.

"If God's so powerful, why doesn't He just make the bad things go away?" The words materialized from Tess's mind, and she bit down hard on her lower lip.

"I can't answer that question. But I do know that time did teach me about faith. Adversity tends to do that; it forces us to sink our roots deep into God's faithfulness or we'll surely topple over."

"Then God let Edgar be destroyed in order for what? To make your faith stronger?"

"I don't know what His purpose was; I will never know until I speak with Him personally. But the experience did make me stronger."

"But your husband's name was cleared too late."

"Perhaps. But if it had been cleared earlier, we wouldn't have moved here, wouldn't have had those *wonderful* years together. We'd have kept working day and night, wasting more time on the pursuit of fame and earthly possessions than on being together." She smiled. "Everything that we work so hard for will either be used up, discarded, or belong to someone else someday. It's a sobering realization, isn't it? I think the reason I had occasional doubts was because Edgar and I had taken too little time to get to know each other. Here, in this beautiful paradise, we were given that time. What a precious gift!"

Tess picked up a throw pillow and held it tightly to her chest. Inside, her emotions churned. What would it be like to trust so implicitly that the outcome didn't matter? To rest so completely in another person's—or deity's—love that the outcome simply wouldn't matter? Something deep inside her twisted—and ached for such a belief.

"You find trust very difficult, don't you, my dear?" Stella gently stoked Henry's fur. "Once I felt the same, but I wish I could help you know the peace that comes from trust—trusting with all your heart."

"Faith and trust weren't Nelson family values," Tess admitted.

"I'm sorry to hear that." Stella's features softened. "We can't pick our parents; we can only become wiser as adults."

Tess straightened, pitching the pillow aside.

"I think I'll see if Carter needs my help."

Stella smiled, reaching for the teapot. "You do that, dear. Perhaps God has provided this time for the two of you to become better acquainted."

14

"We'll be dry in here." Carter opened the door as she ducked into the garage, where stacks of plywood littered the floor. He had managed to get all the boards put up along the back and sides of the house, but the wind made the work difficult, pushing against the plywood as he carried it out. Turning around, his eyes registered her comical attire. Stella had lent her Edgar's old coveralls. They dragged on the floor by a good four inches, and the seat drooped practically to her knees.

"They're not a fashion statement, but they'll help keep you dry," the old woman had promised.

Carter smirked and turned back to his work. He gave a pull on the generator's cord. It roared to life. After a few minutes he turned it off. "That's ready, should we need it." He glanced up at her, then motioned to a paint can on the concrete floor. "Best seat in the house."

She took a discarded rag and dusted off the top before she sat down. Dried pink spatters lined the rim of the bucket. Rain hammered the tile roof, but the shelter's interior felt almost cozy compared to the chaos outside.

"How's Stella?"

"She's holding up okay. She seems pretty calm about all this."

She stared at dark stains dotting the concrete floor. "I don't understand why she's treating the storm so lightly. She doesn't seem concerned about the house, and she knows how destructive hurricanes can be."

"Maybe she's lived through enough storms that she has a sixth sense about the danger—though it's risky reasoning. Older people feel a need to protect their homes . . ." his words trailed off.

Carter sat down on the cold cement beside her. The dampness made dark curls in his hair.

She found herself staring at him. "Naturally curly hair?"

Carter's face turned bright crimson. He leaned to wipe a streak of wet hair off her cheek. The simple, innocent gesture warmed her.

They listened to the roar of the waves. Then Tess's halting voice emerged from the fading daylight, "Did you know that Stella's husband was blacklisted by the McCarthy hearings?" She told him about Edgar, and the injustice that had befallen him and Stella in the late fifties.

"Edgar was a strong man," she concluded. "Or maybe he wasn't. He died too soon still thinking that his name was besmirched."

"I imagine that he knows," Carter said quietly as gusts of wind and rain battered the small garage.

When she remained quiet, he reached over and tugged her pant leg. "You don't agree?"

"If you're implying that he was a Christian so therefore today he is in heaven . . . I think I'd be a little bitter, if I were Edgar."

"And how would bitterness enrich your life?"

She shrugged.

"You're a tough nut to crack, Nelson. Bitterness destroys *you*—not the thing or person you're bitter against."

She reached over and yanked his earlobe playfully. "More Christian philosophy?"

He grinned and lay back, cradling his head in crossed arms. She and Carter fell silent—the nice kind of shared silence that didn't produce a need to talk. After awhile he said, "I guess I should be out there hammering plywood again. Only four windows to go. Care to help me haul these boards?"

"I guess so." She couldn't see how he was going

to get the wood up in gale winds. Carter hummed as he gathered up his supplies for another round of hammering.

Lulled by the sound of rain striking the roof and the soft timbre of Carter's voice, she closed her eyes. The camaraderie between them was nice, more than nice. Trusting. She had enjoyed few such relationships.

Wind snapped a branch and the limb shattered a windowpane. She jumped and scooted closer.

"What's wrong—the glass didn't get you, did it?" Carter shouted above the roar of the storm.

"No—don't you have a flashlight?" Darkness was quickly approaching. They had gotten all but this last piece of plywood in place. At least the board would keep out the rain until the glass could be replaced.

"Yes—somewhere."

He scooted around, trying to locate the object. Eventually his hand closed around the aluminum and he crawled back to her. Switching on the light, he pointed the beam in her eyes. She pulled it out of his hand and directed it at the hole in the glass. "Let's get this up fast," she said, grabbing the corner of the piece of plywood and wrestling it into place. Carter quickly pounded nails into the four corners first before adding a few more along the sides. When he was done he looked over at her rain-soaked face. "What's wrong?" he said, pulling her inside the house.

"Okay. I'm scared. Happy?"

"Delirious." He shifted back to show her a cheesy grin. "What's not to be happy about? We're in a hurricane. We've had nine days of nothing but whale watching, luau's, and—hey—did you get your picture taken with the parrot? The one that digs his claws into your shoulder and draws blood?"

"I missed that."

His playfully drew her closer and in a mock conspiratorial whisper said, "Now tell Carter what Tess is afraid of. Wind?"

"I hate storms, and no, I . . . I don't like wind. I was in a tornado once. I—I can't stand the sound of wind—"

"Yeah, well. I don't like wind, either. But together we'll ride this thing out."

She rested her head on his shoulder and closed her eyes for just a moment. Oddly enough she felt better. Tomorrow she would regret this spurt of idiocy, but right now she was going with it.

"Have you seen the movie *The Perfect Storm*?" she ventured.

He gave her a wry look. "Chatting about *The Perfect Storm* right now makes about as much sense as United Airlines featuring an airline disaster movie on their transatlantic flights." He squeezed her shoulders. "We're taking proper precautions, and now we turn it over to—"

"God." Her defensive tone was gone. For the first time in her life she started to believe it. Carter smiled that broad, beaming smile of his.

"How many children are there in your family?" she asked, suddenly wanting to know more about him.

"I have an older sister. No other siblings."

"I have a younger brother. What's your favorite dessert?"

"Cheesecake—with red stuff swirled through it."

"Lemon pie."

"*Lemon* pie?"

"That's my favorite. School?" she asked.

"Hmm?"

"Where did you go to school?"

"High school—Chicago. Graduated from Baylor University in Waco, Texas. Business major."

"DePauw; Indiana. Master's degrees in finance and psychology."

He let out a low whistle. "Two? As suspected, you're an overachiever."

"What about your grades?"

"They were okay. Dean's list every semester."

"Dean's list is better than 'okay.' What kind of car do you drive?"

"What's this interrogation all about?"

"Nothing." She was suddenly defensive. "I thought since we've become part of each other's lives in the last nine days we should know something about each other."

Carter gently released her gaze and pushed to his feet. "We better see what Stella's up to." He looked through the small opening he had left in the window. The fury intensified.

She lifted her voice. "Is it the hurricane?"

"I'd say," Carter said. "By the looks of things, the eye isn't going to miss us by much."

"It's really kicking up out there," Carter said when he and Tess came into the living room after going to their separate quarters to dry off. With the storm's approach, Stella had insisted he take one of the other guest rooms inside the main house so he wouldn't get doused every time he had to pop into his room. They found Stella sitting peacefully in a chair, feeding Henry pieces of dry Eukanuba.

Tess shook her head in amazement. Neighbors and business owners had battened down hatches and headed for Up Country days ago. Yet Stella calmly fed her cat tiny pieces of food, indifferent to nature's mugging.

She followed Carter into the kitchen, where he switched on the radio and scanned the range of the dial, looking for up-to-the-minute weather advisories. She bent to listen over his shoulder.

He frowned. "Will you stop that—you're putting gray hairs on my head."

Stella smiled gently when Tess paced back into the living room. "Rest, child. Have faith that God is in His kingdom and all is right with the world."

She came to sit down on the sofa. The wind had become a shrieking woman bent on murderous revenge. "Did you have faith?" she asked, trying to take her mind off the storm. "When your husband was accused of being a communist and couldn't work?"

Stella smiled. "Not at first. I remember nights that he was gone to meetings. I assumed they were about scripts. They could have been something else. I never asked. I was selfishly involved in my own career." She gently lowered Henry to the floor. "You see, I never really completely believed Edgar. Some bit of gossip, a thoughtless word, speculative innuendo always made me think that perhaps he'd fallen in with someone, attended some sort of meeting, maybe had done something innocently that had somehow connected him to the Communist Party. I felt there had to be a 'reason' for Jack Warner fingering him as a Communist sympathizer.

"So I waffled between my husband's guilt and innocence. But then I realized there was nothing I could do about any of it if Edgar were guilty. What was happening was out of my hands. When my husband lost his job, we began to lose possessions—things that had meant much to us. We lost our home in Los Angeles. Friends. I began to lose opportunities. Scripts stopped coming. Worse, the rejection was a cancer on Edgar's soul."

Tess reached for a throw pillow and held it on her lap. "Go on."

A smile lit the old woman's eyes. "God knew what we needed. This house—" Stella's gaze swept the room, "was my mother's. When she died, she left it to me. By then Edgar and I had nothing, so you can imagine how much we appreciated getting it."

"You'd lost everything?"

"We lost possessions. But possessions are only things. We lost nothing of value. We still had each another and eventually Mother's house came to us. We both still believed in God."

"Was faith enough when Edgar died?"

"Nothing is enough when you lose the one you love most in the world—not at first," Stella said gently. "But without my strong conviction that ours was only a temporary parting, I would have died with Edgar." Stella's gaze drifted away, and she quietly excused herself to go to her room.

Tess heard Carter switch off the kitchen radio. She got up to rejoin him.

"This thing is going to get a whole lot worse before it gets better," he said grimly.

15

"... moving offshore now. Dangerous storm ... stay tuned for updates ..."

Wind shrieked as Stella serenely adjusted Henry more comfortably around her neck. "I've never left this house in a storm, and I don't plan to start now. But if you kids would feel more secure, go. Drive to Kula. I have a friend there who would be willing to let you sit out the storm with her."

"I think we *all* need to move to a public shelter," Carter said.

Tess could hear a television commentator's sober voice repeating evacuation instructions. Stella couldn't stay here—not alone.

The old woman shook her head. Tess brushed by her and entered the living room. "What's that pounding sound?"

Carter inclined his head, and then proceeded to

the front door, calling back to her, "Someone's here."
Air pressure pushed the door in the moment Carter
turned the knob. Rain came in gusting blasts. Stella
appeared in the hallway, eyes curious. "Fredrick?"
Her smile widened when she spotted the rain-
drenched couple huddled together on the porch.
Both man and woman were stoop-shouldered with
wet gray hair peeking out from beneath yellow rain
slickers. "Ben! Esther!" she called out. "Come in!
Come in! It's a wonder you didn't blow away out
there!"

The elderly couple stepped inside the foyer, greeting Stella warmly. The man extended an arthritic
hand as rain made muddy puddles on the marble
entryway. Stella made the introductions. "Ben and
Esther Grantham, this is Tess Nelson and Carter
McConnell, my houseguests."

Carter shook the white-haired gentleman's hand.
"Tess was just asking Stella if we shouldn't move to
higher ground."

The man's wizened features creased. "It could be
more dangerous getting to shelter now than staying
put. Esther and I have been through some pretty
rough ones. We'd stay at our own place except we're
so close to the shore. The wind took out a big tree in
our yard. It crashed into our dining room. We didn't
figure it was a good idea to just let it pummel us."

His gaze roamed the darkened living room. "Looks like you got this place buttoned up tight. Do you mind if we keep you company until the storm blows over?"

"Of course, you're welcome to stay, Ben." Stella led the couple into the kitchen, motioning for them to sit at the table. "Carter got all the windows covered, so we're nice and cozy in our little cocoon. When the fury worsens we'll have to move to an inside wall of the bathroom."

Tess's stomach hit the floor. *Worsens?* Crashing noises—like a garbage truck dumping a load of glass—thudded outside the windows. Then the noise switched to one of a freight train running through the beach house.

"Thank you, Stella." The old gentleman reached out and ruffled Henry's belly, then seated his wife in a chair adjacent to Stella's. Worry hovered on Esther's matronly face.

"Goodness—it is getting bad." Esther's eyes darted to the window when the sound of a limb snapping and hitting the side of the house crashed.

Tess watched with something like envy as Ben patted his wife's shoulder.

The small group sat in the candlelit room, waiting. Inside Tess, an emotional storm built—a hurricane of circumstances. Nine days ago her biggest worry had been Len Connor; now she was afraid for her life. When asked a week ago what she valued most she would have answered justice. Right now, what she wanted most was another few years—another sunrise. An opportunity to make something of her life, something lasting and worthwhile. She could find another job; she could blot Len and Connor.com out of her mind and put them where they belonged in her priorities. What mattered were the people in her life, her family. As much as she had tried to deny it and had let the bitterness of her childhood blot it out, the truth was she loved her family. She had chosen to remember only the bad times, but there had been good times, too. Sunday afternoons reading the paper together, laughing at the funnies. She had been so preoccupied with finding someone to blame for the downward spiral in her life, she'd forgotten to look for the good. Sure, the bad times had been just as real, but it hadn't all been bad. As she sat here with the wind threatening to blow their house in, it became crystal clear to her. It was Mona she had to contend with—Mona she had to tackle head-on before she could ever resolve the real tempest in her life.

16

Around midnight Ben and Esther started to nod off. Stella and Henry dozed in a nearby chair.

Carter nudged Tess's leg with his foot. "Hanging in there?"

The wind shrieked loudly in the eaves. She looked nervously toward the roof and placed a hand on her stomach.

Carter rested his head against the rim of the sofa and listened as flying objects struck the shuttered windows. Something hard thumped the side of the house, and in the distance storm sirens wailed. He envisioned himself in a war zone, his face white as he ducked reflexively every time a foreign object slammed into the house. Trash receptacles weren't SCUD missiles, but at the moment Carter couldn't distinguish the difference.

He smiled, studying Tess's worried features. She

was a pretty woman, who had a lot to offer a man if she would only release the bitterness in her heart. Carter wasn't usually impulsive; it took him six months to get to know the average woman and even then he moved with caution, but there was something different about this woman.

A nonbeliever.

Was God testing his resolve to follow Him all the way?

Tess shifted and moved closer to the sofa. She seemed almost like a fragile kitten who would look up at him with those doleful eyes, something he could drape around his neck for the rest of his life. Carter shook his head at the thought.

He'd known this woman nine days . . . nine mind-boggling, problematic days, and something was happening inside of him, something bothersome. She was intelligent and goal-oriented; and she couldn't trust anyone if her life depended on it. God, man—the recipient didn't seem to matter. She was incapable of placing her trust in anyone.

Therein lay a major problem; Carter believed that eternal life, and his personal security, hinged on nothing less than the ability to trust.

Trust wasn't concrete—an object that he could hold in his hand and claim ownership of. He had to work at trust as hard as manning his command station, but willingness—the desire to believe—made faith possible.

Oh, Lord Almighty, blessed is the man who trusts in You.

He absently stroked his hand across the top of Tess's hair. The fragrant mass felt soft and smelled of wind and rain.

Her sleepy voice drifted up. "When this is over . . . will you call me?"

Carter smiled, burying his face into the floral silk. "Sure. What shall I call you?"

He could feel her laughing. "Beautiful would be nice." She twisted to look up at him. "No commitment, you understand. But I'd like it if you could call to say hello once in a while, let me know how you are—if those new runways point toward Denver."

"I'd like that. And if you think about it, you can give me a ring every now and then."

She didn't miss a beat. "What sort of ring do you want?"

A smile caught the corners of his mouth. Flirting. They were flirting, and it felt good. "Is this where I'm supposed to say 'a wedding ring'?"

She twisted her body to meet his eyes. "Of course not—"

His tone sobered. "I won't forget this vacation."

Her gaze softened. "Nor will I."

The moment stretched. Finally, she eased free of his embrace, as if she knew that the moment and the relationship were fleeting. "I'm hungry."

Was he glad she'd broken the mood? Maybe. Relieved? Yes.

The only thing he knew for certain was that the relationship wasn't going anywhere—she wasn't a Christian—and the thought stung.

"Nelson? When this is over I'll buy you a sixteen-ounce steak at Moose McGillicuddy's."

"Deal." They shook hands on it.

According to Carter, she didn't have faith because she'd never asked for it.

Just ask for it. Desire it.

Right.

She buttered a piece of bread. Two a.m. approached; the eye of the storm was near.

She was a businesswoman. If a customer didn't place an order, then according to Carter's theory, the customer didn't know they wanted something.

Salvation couldn't be compared to ordering floor wax, but she knew the difference.

Did faith work that way? It sounded too pat—too easy—and in her world, when something sounded "too good to be true" it generally was.

She was savvy enough to know that those professing faith did not live trouble-free lives. If that were the case, then Carter would have had a perfect vacation. He wouldn't be sitting in a stranger's kitchen, eating cold bread and jelly while Maui was getting blown away—or sounded like it.

"Suppose," she mused, setting the bread sack in front of Carter. "Suppose I buy into your theory. My grandmother had faith, but Mona turned out awful. Why would God allow my mother to not inherit her mother's faith?"

"God isn't Santa Claus. Mona had her own choices to make." He offered the spoon, and she licked the remains of the sticky sweetness.

She took a bite of her meal. "Is that what you really think?"

"I think someone you loved very deeply disappointed you," Carter said, taking a bite of his bread also. "I think they broke a trust, and now you find it hard to believe in anyone or anything."

Her jaw dropped. Then she clamped it shut. Tightness formed around her eyes. "You can't know that."

"No, I can't. But you asked me what I thought. I

think that's why you work so hard—you figure since you can't trust anyone to help you, you have to do it all on your own—the perfect career, the perfect life. . . ." He lowered his gaze to the counter. "I'm sorry. I have no right," he said.

Tess had always been cognizant of her need for security. She'd accumulated quite a bit for her age. Stella's earlier words flashed through her mind. *Everything you own will be discarded, used up, or belong to someone else.*

Sure she had a nice apartment, nice furnishings, made some good, solid investments, a healthy 401(k). She'd worked hard for what she had. She had never thought she could take it with her. She wasn't that naïve. Maybe she'd thought that her children would be the benefactors of her hard work, but then, she had no marriage prospects, no plans for children. So, what if the worst happened? What if Alana claimed her life? What would the long hours, pressure, incessant travel have done for her? Wasted her life?

Fierce winds pounded the sheets of plywood nailed across windows, and rain poured rivers through gut-

ters. The restless hurricane seemed intent on showing its true force of power. The sea responded with a
show of uncompromising strength as it hurled brutal
waves against the battered shoreline.

Tess awoke around five a.m. from a brief nap and
lay listening to the wind. Her stomach churned when
she thought of being devoured by the angry sea. But
a short distance away, Carter lay sleeping on the
floor, strong and solid, a symbol of comfort. How had
he managed to penetrate her heart in so short a time?
His words of faith echoed like a voice in a canyon,
resounding until her soul couldn't help but feel com-
pelled to reply. It wasn't a strong answer. No. It was
more a faint whisper, but it came nonetheless and
reverberated through her soul. She wanted the desire
Carter spoke of, the desire to believe. Now the only
question was, how did she get this peace?

With the morning, the storm began to blow itself
out. The ruthless winds calmed as the day lifted its
head from behind gray clouds.

"Looks like it's about over," Ben said from the
front door. His perceptive eyes scanned the after-
math of destruction. "The old houses stood the test
yet another time."

Carter walked to the doorway and stood for a
moment, listening. "Silence," he said.

Outside, distant voices sounded up and down

the beach. Residents had started to come out of houses.

Tess stretched lazily, then touched the small of her back. The floor was hard as a brick. "Is it really over?" She combed her fingers through her tangled hair.

"It's stopped raining and the winds have let up."

When they stepped out onto the patio a moment later, they were greeted with the sight of downed trees. Palm fronds carpeted the saturated ground. In the driveway, a power line hung, snakelike, over her rental car.

"Oh no, look at that," she said. "Do you suppose it hurt the car mechanically?"

Carter squinted cautiously at the line. "I don't know, but we'd better stay clear until we know for sure the power's off."

Turning their backs on the car, she and Carter headed out to inspect the beach. Stella was already out walking, Ben and Esther leading the way.

Debris covered a large area. A mattress floated lazily in the water. Sheets of plywood and dead sea life littered the shore. Tess spotted a New York Yankees hat, the lid to a blender, and a shower cap. One beach house's upper triangular walls had blown in. Carter picked his way among felled birds and fish tossed onto the shore while she followed close behind. Numerous buildings were blown down. A pair of men's pants hung in a palm tree. Briefly she closed her eyes to block out the vision of ruin. Where hours ago shopkeepers and tourists had bought and sold souvenirs and macadamia nuts, now the seaside town of Kihei looked like a war zone.

"And what, fair lady, shall we do on this tenth day of our lovely vacation?" Carter paused to stare at a beach chair bobbing in the ocean, his tone light but his eyes serious. "Want to try for ten pipers piping?"

"Naw, the nine drummers drove me nuts." She regrouped and matched his tone. "But there's still so much we haven't done, Carter! Earthquakes, locust plagues, aviation disasters—"

Mentally, she began to rehearse the catalog of folly that had been her "vacation." "Let's see what we *did* manage to accomplish—my cab had a blowout on the way to Stapleton. I had to run to make the flight and I turned my ankle in the process."

"So? I had a miserable cold and my ears killed me on the flight over." Carter stood poised for the battle of who-had-the-worst-vacation.

"Oh, how sad!" She grinned as the tension of the past hours gradually released. Alana had left behind destruction, but the storm had spared the island residents—she'd heard no report of death or serious injury. "You didn't have cold pills in your luggage?"

"I didn't *have* luggage by that time."

"But you could have bought some Sudafed when you arrived at your hotel."

"Oh, by then I had my luggage back."

"You did?"

"Oh yeah. Only the hotel burned down, and I lost it again."

"Oh, that hotel!" She was enjoying their game. "I was staying there. Pioneer Inn? Lovely historical place. When I had to vacate the room, I grabbed my makeup bag instead of my purse."

"Go figure."

"Then I spent half the day running around dressed in a blanket."

He viewed her with mock surprise. "You're *that* woman?"

She sobered as her eyes skimmed the storm damage. It would take Kihei months to recover, but the little seaside town had heart. She remembered Beeg—safely in New York. What would Beeg do if she came home to find her gallery destroyed and her watercolors ruined?

Every earthly possession will be used up, given away, or belong to someone else.

She sighed. Carter reached out for her hand and she for his. "Heck of a vacation, Ms. Nelson. Who's your travel agent?"

She paused, then admitted, "Actually I was thinking your travel agent looks a little more . . . trustworthy."

The damage to Stella's house was appreciable. Tiles had blown off the roof, shutters were damaged beyond repair. Downed tree limbs scattered the lawn. Snakes, insects, and rodents driven to higher ground were everywhere—causing more than a little anxiety for cleanup crews. Carter and Tess skirted puddles as they returned to the beach house. Carter coughed hollowly.

He smiled at her concerned look. "I need hot coffee. Lots of coffee."

Ben, Esther, and Stella were still down the beach inspecting damage. They had the house to themselves. Pouring two cups of coffee, Carter sat down at the table.

Tess remained at the window, arms crossed, staring out.

"Coffee's getting cold."

"I don't want coffee."

He poured cream into his cup and stirred. "What do you want, Tess? Do you know?"

"How does anyone really know what they want?" she asked, her gaze still outside the one window Carter had freed from its plywood imprisonment.

"I suppose they don't," Carter said quietly. "Not without serious thought about what's important to them."

"I want to trust in God like you do," she admitted. "But how do I do that?"

"A child stands on the edge of a swimming pool and says, 'Daddy! Catch me!' and jumps almost before the words are out of his mouth. How does he know his daddy will catch him?"

"Because he always had caught him?"

"Childlike faith. The unwavering trust in his father, knowing that he's never dropped him, never failed to catch him. That's what faith in God is all about."

Her top teeth worried her bottom lip. "I'm going home, Carter."

He glanced up. His eyes darkened at the announcement. "There won't be any flights out for a few hours."

"I know—but when there are I'm going back to Denver. I need to know that I'm not just feeling this way because of the strain of the storm. . . . I don't want to be a Christian in hard times. If this is real and true, it needs to be for always. I need to go home and think. . . ."

Shoving back from the table, Carter said quietly, "Then as soon as the airport opens we'll get you a flight."

Around eight o'clock, an employee from Pioneer Inn arrived. Rapping on the door, he stood on the back porch and waited. Tess spotted him through the kitchen window. Lifting the sill, she called, "May I help you?"

"Tess Nelson?"

She frowned. "I'm Tess."

The boy waved an envelope. "This came for you day before yesterday. Sorry, because of the storm this was the soonest I could get here."

Drying her hand on a towel, she went to open the door. When she looked inside the envelope, she found a voucher for five hundred dollars and a note from Mona.

Life hasn't been easy without Roy; money is always tight. I will need the cash back as soon as you can repay it. Mona.

Tess felt hot tears sting her eyes. She'd sent the money. Mona had not let her down. For the first time in her life, Mom had come through.

Her throat ached from the lump of emotion suddenly blocking her windpipe.

17

A power company crew working the area late Sunday night removed the line from Tess's rental car. Unfortunately, the jolt of power from the line had zapped the car's electronic ignition system, leaving the vehicle undriveable. Stella immediately offered her the use of her battered truck.

After stowing her soot-covered bags in the back of the Chevy pickup Monday morning, Carter climbed into the driver's seat. Air traffic out of Kahului Airport had resumed operation. Main throughways had been cleared of power lines and debris.

Stella carried Henry in her arms as she walked Tess out to the truck. "I know you want to go home. You have choices to make about your job, and I trust you will make those decisions wisely. But I have so much enjoyed knowing you, having you here." She smiled fondly at Carter. "Both of you. You are welcome in my home any time. And I pray the Lord will return you someday to Maui—preferably under more pleasant conditions. The island really is paradise, you know."

Tess smiled though tears stung her eyes. The former movie queen turned to address Carter, "Now, young man, you are to spend the remainder of the afternoon with me. I'll have Fredrick prepare us a nice fruit tray—the pineapple is extra sweet this year—"

The old woman turned as a white-haired gentleman rounded the corner of the house. She broke into a beam. "Fredrick!"

Tess gaped at Carter.

"Stella, my dear." The distinguished gent dressed in a white suit and spats—yes, spats—bent to place a succinct kiss on each of Stella's red-rouged cheeks. "I have been so worried about you. I trust you made it through the storm without any real harm?" His eyes lifted to curiously size up the two strangers.

Stella introduced Tess and Carter and explained how they had come to stay with her.

"The Lord was with us, Fredrick. And my new friends have been with me all the time—and Ben and Esther."

"I am so relieved to know that Stella had someone

to keep her company," Fredrick confessed as he shook Carter's hand. "I wanted to call, but heavy trade winds took my phone lines down two days ago."

"Good to meet you, Fredrick." Carter grinned. "Tess and I were beginning to wonder if you really existed."

"Oh, indeed I do, kind sir. Indeed I do." With a snap of his heels, Fredrick bowed. "If you will excuse me, I must see to the house, and Stella's lunch."

Draping an arm around Stella's waist, Tess steered her new friend to the passenger side of the cab. "You've been wonderful to both Carter and me. I wish I knew how to thank you."

"Oh, my dear, it is I who should be thanking you. You and Carter have brought sunshine into my life— even in the midst of a storm." For a split second, Stella embraced her. "You will stay in touch? Perhaps give an old lady a call occasionally?"

Tess enfolded her fragile frame and hugged her tightly. "I promise."

As Carter backed the truck out of the drive, Stella suddenly quickened her steps. Her eyes deepened with concern. Reaching out, she grasped onto her fingers through the open window. Tess held on tightly.

"Remember the things we talked about," Stella called. "About trust, and faith and love."

"I will." She knew that she would never forget the time she'd spent in Stella's house, or the long talks and the woman's wisdom. She swiped at tears stinging her eyes.

The Chevy was old and rattled as if it would fall apart. Carter seemed unusually quiet, Tess assumed because he was concentrating on driving. Or was he avoiding conversation? The air between them was charged, as if they both had something weighing on their minds and neither could push past politeness to speak. His stern features indicated that he was troubled. Maybe he thought that rushing back to Denver would only cast her back into the same mold she'd always been in. And perhaps that could happen, but she didn't think so. Ever since she'd gotten the telegram and money from her mother a new thought had been forming within her. Now, as they made their way along the cluttered, storm-strewn streets of Kihei, she saw with clarity why she'd always held back, had been so terrified of trusting. Mona. The one person she'd tried so hard to trust, who had invariably failed her, finally came through, and with that one act, Tess felt her foundations shake. If Mona, who was far from perfect, could be trusted, perhaps God, the God Carter loved so dearly, deserved her trust, too. But first she had to go to Indiana, to see her mother for herself. Indiana held the key to her problems.

She looked over at Carter. The thought of never seeing him again left her hurting. Somehow it seemed wrong to walk away from this man; why, her practical side couldn't fathom. But like the air she breathed, it just was.

Carter peered at the vacillating dash gauges, seemingly unaware of the turmoil going on inside her. "The gas gauge is sticking. Stella and Fredrick must not believe in maintenance." His voice fell to silence.

She studied the pineapple fields as the old truck rattled along Highway 30. She was heading home; Carter was going back to Chicago and his job at O'Hare—his church work. She recalled the dedication in his voice when he spoke of his mission trips to faraway places like Bosnia, El Salvador, and his newest project, an orphanage in Uganda. How she wished she could do something so noble, so *meaningful* with her life.

Her eyes switched to the Bible lying on the seat between them. She picked it up and glanced over questioningly. Carter turned the wheel, and they headed down 380. His jaw locked, and she wondered if she'd aggravated him by handling the book. Even he would have to admit that not everybody carried a Bible in their front seat. Maybe Jehovah's Witnesses . . . pastors.

Carter answered her silent inquiry. "I've fallen behind on my reading lately."

She lightly skimmed the worn pages. Passages were highlighted in yellow; notations made to the side.

She closed the Bible. "If the Bible is the best-selling book in the world, what's the second?"

He shook his head. "I have no idea."

"Would you think I'm full of myself if I told you that I knew?"

He glanced at her.

"Well, I don't—I haven't a clue either," she admitted lightly, "but I do know the Bible sells over a million copies a year—read that in a Crimson and Brown report. Why that particular fact was mentioned in a human resource periodical, I can't imagine." She lifted the heavy black book again and stared at it. "Have you read this through?"

"Several times."

She lifted her eyebrows. "Several times? Why? Does it update itself?"

"No, it doesn't change—only my comprehension changes. Every time I read it, I discover something I didn't know before."

She could see she was getting to him. He gripped the steering wheel, staring straight ahead. Not the relaxed Carter of days past. He seemed on edge, tense. Distant. Well, maybe that was what she wanted: distance. The relationship had all the signs of . . . what? Turning serious? Hardly. After today she would most likely never see him again.

She laid the book back on the seat between them.

He turned to focus on her. "Are you sure you aren't leaving for different reasons?"

"Like what?"

"Maybe you're afraid."

"Afraid!" she scoffed. "Of what?"

"I don't know." Carter turned onto the exit. "Afraid of discovering that God loves you more than you can imagine."

"Why would that frighten me?"

"Love is a terrifying thing—it gives, yes. But it asks a lot more in return. You'd have to give up everything for Him—for Jesus. A lot of people turn back because of that. You'd have to let go of your unholy twins."

"Unholy twins?"

"Hurry and worry."

"Hurry and worry," she repeated. "Whatever."

"You hurry too much, and you're going to worry yourself into an early grave."

"Now just one minute—"

"*Face* it, Tess. That's why you're in such an all-fired hurry to leave Maui. You can't stand the thought of rejection, that Len Connor fired you. You can't wait to get back and have the last say."

His observation stung, and he couldn't be more off base. Well, maybe there was a grain of truth in the accusation, but who was he to butt into her personal life?

"Quite obviously you don't live in the same world I do, Mr.-Perfect-Carter-McConnell. Worry is a natural extension of any high-pressure job."

"You can't say my job isn't high pressure," he reminded her.

"And you couldn't take the stress—you said so earlier. The only reason you came to Maui was because you were forced to slow down. So don't talk to me about hurry and worry. Those *twins* are on your back, too!" She could feel her blood pressure boiling. Then she added insult to injury. "Plus, you have it *easy*, Carter. You aren't upwardly mobile like I am. You've reached your goals."

"Have I, now?"

"Haven't you? You sit in a tower, directing planes to safe landings and takeoffs."

When he refused to capitulate, she baited, "Isn't that true? You've already reached your potential?"

"My potential won't be reached until I see Jesus face to face."

She crossed her legs and her arms. One foot twitched erratically.

She sobered as the years fell away, and she once

again squirmed beside her grandmother in a pew as the priest's words filled the large sanctuary.

"Are you far more valuable to Him than the birds of the air? Can all your worries add a single moment to your life?"

"The Jewish have a saying," Carter's voice broke into her suddenly melancholy reverie. "'Worms eat you when you're dead. Worry eats you when you're alive.' Worry erodes the machinery of our lives. Faith and trust are the grease that keeps it running smoothly."

She felt helpless to argue. Memories had stripped her of self-assurance; confidence momentarily deserted her. Passages long forgotten drifted back to her.

"Look at the lilies and how they grow. They don't work or make their clothing, yet Solomon in all his glory was not dressed as beautifully as they are. And if God cares so wonderfully for flowers that are here today and gone tomorrow, won't He more surely care for you?"

"I don't understand God," she admitted. "I just don't. But—you're going to have to trust *me*—I want to. I really do."

Carter reached for her hand and held it tightly.

A few minutes later his "Uh, oh," broke the silence.

"What's the matter?"

The engine sputtered, then coughed. She glanced

at the gas gauge as the old wheezer started to buck. "Don't tell me we're out of gas!"

The Chevy rumbled and spat a couple more times. Carter swerved the vehicle to the edge of the road. "Okay," Carter agreed, "but somebody needs to inform you."

Panic crowded the back of her throat. *Out of gas?* The truck was out of *gas* and she had a flight out in one hour? Her eyes darted, trying to locate a nearby gas station.

Carter switched off the ignition. "I'll bet nobody's put gas in the tank in months." He opened the door and unfolded his long legs out of the cab. "We passed a convenience store half a mile back."

She went on point. "You have to walk? How long will that take?"

"I don't know. I'm not an Olympic sprinter, but I'll be back as soon as I can."

She scooted across the seat and shouted after his retreating back. "My plane leaves in *one* hour, Carter! It will take me that long to get through security!"

"I'm aware of when your plane leaves, Tess."

Carter trekked back to where they'd come from while she kept track of his progress through the back window. It didn't take long for the truck's cab to heat up. She wished she'd dressed a little more casually. Her nylons were already sticking to her legs.

She thought about getting out of the truck and standing somewhere cooler. She opened the truck door, hoping to catch a breeze. Twenty minutes passed. Finally she slid out of the truck and paced the side of the road.

About the time she decided something awful had happened to Carter and he was never coming back, a rattletrap truck sped down the road and skidded to a halt beside her. Carter clambered out and lifted a gas can from the truck's bed.

"Thanks!" he called.

"Aloha!" a voice returned before the truck sped off.

Carter lugged the heavy can to the back of the truck and uncapped the tank. Tipping the can, he poured gas into the empty tank. Sweat rolled down the sides of his flushed face. "Relax. You'll make the plane."

Relax. She resumed pacing.

By the time Carter returned the gas can, filled the tank, and parked the truck in "short term" parking, the plane was due to take off in twenty-five minutes. Tess's nerves were raw and stretched to the limit as Carter lugged her bags to the curbside check-in line. Minutes later, after retrieving her boarding pass, she made a break for the gate. Halfway there, she turned around and stopped. Harried passengers swerved around her to avoid a collision.

Carter stood in the opening of the breezeway,

watching her. She hadn't said good-bye. She realized this was the moment she had been avoiding all day.

Turning around, she walked back. They stood for a moment, breathing deeply of tuberose-scented tropical air. Paradise.

Silence stretched. Then he leisurely held out his arms and she walked into them. Holding on tightly, she closed her eyes and savored the last few hints of his cologne. She searched but couldn't find the words to say what she wanted to say. For the past ten days he had been a source of strength and hope that she never knew she needed.

"Thank you," she whispered.

His hold tightened. "You weren't kidding about staying in touch?"

"Do you want me to?"

"I want you to."

She wasn't sure how he kept his voice so calm, so level, when all she wanted to do was cry.

Gently releasing her, he stood back and smiled. "Take care of yourself, Tess Nelson."

"You, too, Carter McConnell." She grinned. Tears stung her eyes as she turned away and walked toward the gate. She heard his voice calling above the noisy room.

"I'm holding you to your promise to call. Don't forget me."

Forget him? Impossible.

Moments later, she raced down the jetway and onto the wide-bodied plane. Breathless, and fighting back tears now, she located her seat. Buckled in, she fumbled for a tissue. She wished she'd never met Carter McConnell—knowing him only added another confusing equation to her messed-up life.

The plane remained unmoving in its place at the gate. Tess thumbed through a copy of *United Airline Promo Magazine* and listened for the door to seal. She checked the time. Back to her magazine.

Thirty minutes had passed when the pilot announced there would be a slight delay.

What *now?* If she could only get *out* of paradise— away from Carter—away from this feeling that because of this Chicago flight controller and his beliefs, her life would never be the same.

Another thirty minutes crept by. Passengers fanned themselves with newspapers; babies cried.

"Ladies and gentleman," the pilot's grave voice came over the intercom. "Sorry about the delay. Seems there's been a security breach. Passengers will have to deplane."

She slammed her head solidly back against the seat. Why not? What *ever* made her think she was going to get off the island this easily?

With a sigh of resignation, she picked up her purse and stepped into the aisle.

"How long?" she asked as she passed the flight attendant.

The lady shrugged. "Stay close. The airline will keep you informed."

18

The message light on the answering machine was blinking when Tess turned the key and let herself into the apartment. She glanced at it. Twelve calls. Her thoughts drifted: Len.

He'd taken his good ol' sweet time to call.

After dumping her bags in the bedroom, she returned to the hallway and jacked up the heat. Though the apartment was exactly as she'd left it, the place didn't feel like home anymore. What had changed? Her?

The two-hour delay at Kahului had given her time to reflect on her life and the direction she'd been going. She hadn't cared for the insight. Always the smug career machine, the Tess of the past had attributed success to self-achievement, but vacation . . . and Carter McConnell . . . had made her realize that no man—or woman, for that matter—was an island. Tess Nelson needed help.

She unpacked and then addressed the imminent problem: her phone messages. The first message came on. "Tess . . . ?" It was Len. He sounded contrite—no, penitent. "Tess—sweetie. I tried the hotel in Maui, and the clerk said there'd been some sort of accident—fire—something. Anyway, call me the minute you get home. We need to talk."

Beep.

The lack of genuine concern in Len's message irritated Tess. How about an *"Are you okay? Were you hurt in the fire?"*

Then message two started in. "Okay." It was Len again. "So, Chuck isn't working out as I'd hoped. . . . Are you calling in to hear your messages? . . . Um, call me."

"Hey, Tess." Len again, for the third message. "Look, Babe—we're hurting here—I've been following Alana on the Weather Channel. Looks like she got pretty ugly. Air traffic's resumed—I know you didn't stick around to help with the cleanup, so I know you're back. Where are you? Come on, I'm waiting to hear from you. Things are a mess here. Connor.com needs you."

All in all there were eleven calls from Len, all essentially the same. The twelfth call was from Carter, checking to see that she'd arrived safely. Sweet, unselfish Carter.

Her finger hit delete. She'd waited, had been sure Len would make just such a call, but somehow it didn't satisfy as she'd hoped. There was still a hollowness in the pit of her stomach.

A second later, the doorbell rang. Groaning, she thought about ignoring the intrusion. She was tired, had severe jetlag—the last thing she wanted right now was to relive the events of her vacation in paradise.

Whoever it was leaned on the bell with persistence. Len? He wouldn't dare show up—not without warning her first. When she opened the door, she found her next-door neighbor, Herb Franklin, steadying a large vase of red roses. He smiled when he saw her. "Thank goodness—I thought we had a prowler." His features sobered. "I thought you planned to be away a few more days. I heard someone come in and I came to investigate."

"Lucky criminal," she said as she eyed the voluminous bouquet. And such lovely extravagance—at least three-dozen crimson American Beauty's were arranged with sprigs of baby's breath. "Are those mine?"

Herb handed her the crystal vase. "They came today—and one yesterday just like it, and a similar one the day before." He flashed an apologetic grin. "It will take me a few minutes to get the vases all over here." He turned and trekked back to his residence.

For a fleeting moment she hoped they were from Carter, but just as quickly she realized that would've been impossible since he couldn't very well have sent them when she was still in Hawaii. She opened the card and read the inscription:

We need you, Tess. *Call* me. Len.

At 12:50 a.m. Tess sat up and pitched the heavy comforter aside. Denver streetlight filtered through the bedroom curtain. Tylenol; she needed a pain reliever. The smell of roses was overpowering. A jackhammer pounded in her right temple, and her ankle ached. Even an earlier soak in the whirlpool tub had failed to loosen the tight muscles coiled in her shoulders. Having grown accustomed to the sound of surf breaking along the shoreline, now Tess found herself disturbed by Denver's sirens, the crunch of steel-belted tires on packed snow, and wind howling up the apartment eaves.

Getting out of bed, she crammed her feet into slippers and pulled on her robe. As she walked through the front room, she switched on lamps. The darkness bothered her, the gloom, the uncertainty of what lay in the shadows.

I'm being maudlin, she warned herself as she entered the kitchen and picked up the teakettle and filled it with water. *You're weirding out, Tess.*

Waiting for the water to heat, she sat at the table and peeled an apple, watching the peel grow longer and longer. She was so fascinated by the progression that when the teakettle blasted a shrill whistle she jumped as though someone had fired a cannon through the window.

Moments later she dropped a bag of Lipton in the cup, thinking about Len's earlier messages. *Call me.*

Well, Len, I have called you—everything in my arsenal of bad names.

Propping her chin on her hand, she dunked the bag up and down in hot water and wondered why she didn't feel justified. Cleansed. She had gotten want she'd wanted, hadn't she? Len Conner on all fours. He had called. Her position with Connor.com was waiting to be reclaimed.

With a fat raise and a sizable bonus at year's end, no doubt.

So where was the elation? The thrill of victory?

Life wasn't fair. Wasn't that what Stella had said? And the old movie queen's wisdom was profound.

Her mind flew back to her talks with Stella and

Carter. Hadn't she told Carter that she wanted to finally trust God? Yet she knew that if that was ever going to happen she had to let go of the one thing that held her back—no, the two things, she decided. First, she needed to get over what Len Connor had done, and second, she needed to forgive her mother. She absently stirred the cup of tea as the apple lay forgotten beside the cup.

Starting tomorrow morning, she was going to find the real woman. The real Tess Nelson.

The dilapidated row house stood like a war-weary soldier backlit by the early morning Indiana sky-line. Tess had never come to see her mother with-out calling first, but then this January had been anything but typical for her.

She proceeded up the snow-packed walk. Her breath puffed a frosty vapor in the bitterly cold air. A man wrapped in a shabby-looking overcoat and wearing a fedora exited the building carrying a long-handled shovel. If the tenants wanted snow off their walk it was up to them to remove it. There was no hired help to do it here as there was in her condo.

The man nodded as she passed. Years of bleak existence looked back at her.

"Morning."

"Good morning." She opened the glass door marred by hundreds of handprints and stepped into the foyer. Mailboxes lined the chipped, painted wall; a potted plant that might once have contributed oxygen no longer even tried. Dead leaves gathered in a shallow pool at the base of the cracked terra cotta-colored plastic.

She pressed the elevator button. The cables clicked as the car slowly started its descent to her. Her eyes scanned the squalid conditions, and she was overcome with guilt when she thought about her warm apartment, filled with trendy furniture and Beeg's watercolor prints. How could Mona live here? Steel doors labored open, and Tess waited for the bouncing elevator car to stabilize.

Hesitantly entering the cave, she removed her winter gloves and pressed the sixth-floor button. The tiny room smelled of perspiration and wet dog. She watched the light buttons and thought about how hard it would be for a woman Mona's age to transport heavy sacks of groceries to the sixth floor. She leaned and pressed the button again. Then twice more before the door shut.

Getting off on six, she walked down the long

hallway that reeked of fried meat and burnt toast. She paused in front of Mona's apartment: 607.

Drawing a deep breath, she rapped on the door that held a pink, faded, plastic, floral bouquet on its surface. She could hear Katie Couric and Matt Lauer chatting with Al Roker in the background, something about the unexpected snowfall in the Big Apple that morning.

She listened to the sounds of footsteps and bumps emanating from inside the apartment, as if someone was searching for something to throw on. Shortly the door creaked open a crack and for the first time in sixteen years she met her mother's eyes.

"Mama?"

The door shut as the security chain rattled, and then the door opened fully. Mona stood in front of her with a faded, turquoise, chenille housecoat half off her shoulder, hair poking out of red Velcro curlers. A Winston sagged from the corner of her mouth. Clearly she was surprised to see Tess, though she made some effort to remain unreadable. "Who died?"

Tess managed a wavering smile. "Nobody. I know I should have called, but I . . . thought maybe it's been too long. I should pay a visit in person."

Mona's gaze raked her, and Tess was suddenly self-conscious of her blatant show of affluence compared to her surroundings. Why hadn't she worn jeans and running shoes? Her mother stepped back, motioning her inside. "You don't need more money, do you?" she said.

"No, Mother."

She entered the cubicle of an apartment, her eyes skimming the interior. A closet ran the length of the entryway. Small living room, tiny kitchenette. One bedroom off to the left. At least the bed was made. A stack of books was piled on the end table with pre-scription medicine vials—six of them. A pair of glasses lay open beside them.

A twenty-one-inch television, with what looked to be an ancient Nintendo attached, blared from its perch: a scarred, inexpensive pressed-sawdust table that could be purchased at Kmart and hand assem-bled. Her eyes skimmed the picture taken shortly after Mona and Roy's marriage. She'd seen it through-out her childhood. The photo had been taken in front of a Woolworth's in Texas. A nineteen-year-old Roy was wearing a sailor cap, and sixteen-year-old Mona wore her hair upswept. The smiling couple looked happy.

Once Tess took a seat, Mona closed the door and slid the security chain back into place. "Thought you were in Hawaii."

"I got back day before yesterday."

"Is it nice?" Mona took her coat and draped it

over the back of a kitchen chair. Dishes with dried food cluttered the sink. A skillet of bacon grease congealed on the two-burner stove.

She shrugged. "It's tropical."

"Expensive, I hear."

Tess smiled. At nine dollars a pound for fresh asparagus, she guessed it was safe to say prices were high. "Very."

Shuffling past her, Mona made her way to the frayed sofa. As she passed the table bearing the Nintendo, she switched the television off. A deck of cards in Solitaire order splayed across an aluminum television tray facing the couch. An ashtray, overflowing with butts, lent its evidence to the smoky smell that permeated the tiny quarters.

Grinding out one cigarette, Mona flicked a Bic lighter and lit another one as she studied Tess beneath shaded lids. The years had been cruel to Mona Nelson. Lines etched her leathery skin like erratic road maps, paving the way to eyes shrunken deeply back in her skull.

Tess fished in her purse for the envelope. "I've brought your money back."

"Good." Mona peered at the offering through a veil of blue smoke.

She laid the money on the end table. Silence surpassed the sounds coming from the low-rent housing hallway—someone running a vacuum, an infant crying in the distance.

A child was the product of his environment, that she would agree. Sadly, for the last thirty-two years she had practiced Mona and Roy's belief, lived under the assumption that Christianity was a lie. Yet in the past week she'd come to see that they had been wrong; she had been wrong. She had witnessed not only God's existence but His love for her. She'd seen it in Stella and Carter, in their willingness to reach out to her. Now it was her turn to reach out in forgiveness.

Her eyes scanned the squalor. There had to be a stronger reason for life than this. Tess saw before her a woman who did not need to be feared, but a woman to be pitied. Her heart swelled with a long forgotten love. Mona had lived her whole life in an aura of distrust and desperation. Perhaps her lack of spiritual awakening was a by-product of her own painful childhood. Instinct told Tess that Mona held the key to her emotional restoration, and she knew the key could not turn in the lock without forgiveness and compassion. Mona was sixty-two years old. She lived in an empty world of cigarettes, computer games, and soap operas.

"Is there anything I can do for you—anything you want?"

"No, I do okay. A neighbor lady takes me to the grocery store and to pick up my medicine on Saturdays. I do all right."

"I want to pay your bills each month." She drew a long breath. "Send me the amount you need and I'll send you a check."

"I don't need your charity."

"I know you don't. This is something I want to do."

"Well." She shrugged. "If you have money to burn go ahead."

Tess suddenly bent to give her mother a stiff hug. She felt Mona's hand touch the back of her hair.

"Well," Tess straightened, pasting on a smile, afraid she would cry. "I need to be going."

Mona got up and opened the door. "I suppose there is one thing you could do for me."

"What's that?"

"I'd like to have a PlayStation."

"PlayStation? One of those computer toys?"

She nodded. "Roy's old Nintendo is just about to give out on me. I'd sure enjoy a PlayStation, maybe a few extra games—if that wouldn't be asking too much."

"No— I'll send you a PlayStation when I get back to Denver."

For an instant Tess looked deeply into her

mother's eyes, and she wanted to believe—oh, how she wanted to trust that what she saw in the faded brown gaze was more than regret for lost years, maybe even a hint of love for her.

"Bundle up tight. It's cold out there," Mona said.

She obediently fastened the bottom button on her coat and pulled on warm gloves. "Take care of yourself, Mom."

Mona nodded. "You, too."

19

Airport gift shops were about as personal as a blender for Christmas, but Tess found a stuffed cat that looked a whole lot like Henry. She purchased the cat, and included the toy with a large box of chocolates and had the gifts mailed to Stella along with a note thanking her for her hospitality. Stella had offered more than hospitality; she had offered new insight. Tess had sadly been lacking in that commodity. Stella also offered friendship. Friendships took time to cultivate and nurture. Over the years Tess had worked too many long hours and weekends to develop close relationships. She needed to change that.

As she was paying for the chocolates, her eyes centered on a box of nuts and she thought of Len, whose frantic calls she had yet to return. They would serve as a succinct answer to his pleas for help. *Nuts to you.*

"I'll take a box of nuts, too."

"Certainly." The clerk reached behind her and snagged a five-pound assortment of almond macadamias. "Will there be anything else?"

"Yes. I want to enclose this note with the gift." She scribbled a brief message that read, "Thanks, but not interested. Tess." She handed the card back to the woman. "Will those go out today?"

"Sometime late this afternoon."

"Thanks."

Tess left the shop, pausing outside long enough to blow air out of her cheeks. She still had to send the check for the airline ticket, but it was over.

Man. She gave the air a jubilant right hook. That felt good. *Really good.*

Groundhog Day arrived on the heels of a Denver blizzard. Punxsutawney Phil emerged from his burrow and saw his shadow, so weather forecasters predicted winter would hang around for another six weeks.

Trudging through nine inches of snow with more falling in the mall parking lot, Tess huddled deeper into the lining of her wool coat. By the looks of the empty lot, not many Denverites were out shopping today.

Inside the sprawling Denver Mall complex, Tess stomped snow off her boots and made her way to B. Dalton's bookstore. On the flight home from Indiana two days ago she'd come up with a plan—an "enlighten Tess" strategy. There was no way on earth that she was going to read and understand the King James Bible, but logic said there were other ways to learn about the gospel.

Thirty minutes later she carried her purchases to the counter. She didn't blink when the clerk perused the two titles: *The Complete Idiot's Guide to the Bible* and *No Brainer's Guide to the Bible*.

Back in her own habitat, she shrugged out of her coat and boots and emptied the sack of reading material on the sofa. Wielding a yellow highlighter, she started to read. Noon passed, and she didn't break for lunch.

Late afternoon, she ate a handful of Ritz crackers and some bologna. When she came to a thought or paragraph that she questioned, she highlighted it. Rereading her scribbles she realized that every other line in the first two chapters was highlighted. And this was the easy version.

By nightfall, instead of Dan Rather's voice filtering from her apartment, Tess's mystified exclamations of

"Huh?" and "Oh, now how can that be?" or the occasional "Give me a break" shattered the silence.

But after reading most of the day, she slept better that night than she had in a long time. When she awoke in the night she tried praying. Her novice attempts were halting at first. She prayed about the weather—and Herb Franklin's continuing good health. Stella's name came up once or twice. Carter's more than twice. She felt a sense of peace overtake her, a sense that she was no longer alone. God could be trusted because He loved her—He loved Tess Nelson.

The following morning, she found herself talking out loud as she dumped coffee grinds to make a fresh pot.

That night Carter was still on her mind—she sincerely hoped that he wouldn't look back on his time in Maui and remember Tess Nelson as a nut case who'd spoiled his vacation.

Reaching for the phone, she called Beeg. When her college roommate's voice came on the line, she grinned. "Well, it's about time."

"Tess! Is that you?" Beeg squealed. "I'm so sorry I missed you—when are you coming to Maui again?"

She sank down to the sofa, speechless. "Do I have a story for you."

For over an hour, she told of her exploits and

how she'd weathered Alana in paradise. Bee Gee told her about the damage to her shop—most everything had been lost; insurance covered the building but couldn't come near to the value of her lost artwork.

"Stella DeMuer—the old movie queen? You stayed in Stella DeMuer's beach house?" Beeg exclaimed when Tess told her about her accommodations after the fire.

"She's wonderful, Beeg. Could you go visit Stella sometime? She's so lonely, and you would love her."

"Sure, I've always wanted to see the inside of her home. Does she really wear a cat around her neck?"

"Henry." Tess grinned.

Beeg's tone had softened. "You sound different, Tess. Happier. Have you met someone?"

Had she met someone? Carter's face flashed through her mind. Besides the Lord? "Could be—and I am happier, Beeg. I've been reading the Bible lately."

"Yeah? Me, too! I've been going to church with a guy. You know, there could be something to this religion thing."

"Yeah," Tess agreed. "I think there really could be, Beeg."

That night she dug Carter's home phone number out of her purse and dialed Chicago. She knew the games women were supposed to play—don't be pushy. Wait for him to call. Don't appear too needy.

Well, Carter's and her relationship wasn't Romeo and Juliet's. But she wasn't going to play any games. If he mistook a simple phone call between two acquaintances to be anything other than innocuous, that was his problem. She drummed her fingernails on the end table as she listened to the first ring.

Then two.

Three. Her heart took a nosedive. He wasn't home. She wondered if he'd stayed in Maui. She absently flipped the remote to the Weather Channel.

On the fifth ring, Carter's voice came on the line. "Hello."

Relief flooded her. "Hey. I was about to hang up."

"Hey—is this Tess?"

She sat back on the sofa, closing her eyes. It felt so good to hear his voice. Suddenly it seemed the weight of the world had lifted from her shoulders. "Ms. Unlucky Charm in person."

His tone modulated. "Hi, girl."

"I see you made it back to Chicago."

"Smooth as silk this time. What about you?"

"We had to deplane for a couple of hours because of a security breach—the airlines never said what kind of a breach. After that the flight was uneventful. So, how are things? Back to work yet?"

"Not yet. I'm scheduled for next week, though."

They chatted about nothing. Then about everything. She had forgotten how easy he was to confide in.

"Hey," he said.

"What?"

"When's your birthday?"

"July fourth. Why?"

"No kidding. July fourth? I woke up in the middle of the night last night and remembered you hadn't included that with your address."

She smiled, recalling the night of the hurricane and the candid sharing of their lives as they sat on Stella's cold garage floor.

"When's yours?"

"July fifth."

"No way."

"Why would I lie about my birthday?"

"Well." She debated the next line. The "rules" would strongly advise against it. "Maybe we'll share a birthday cake this year."

"Sounds good to me. I hope you like German chocolate."

"I love chocolate of any nationality."

They laughed.

"I like you, Nelson." This from Carter.

"I like you too, McConnell."

"Exactly when do you think that happened? When I handed you the package of tissues at the airport? Or maybe it was over the luggage carousel when you had such charitable thoughts about my stealing your suitcase."

She felt color dot her cheeks. "I think it was . . . about the time you looked at me as if I'd lost my mind on the hotel fire escape and you had to haul me down two flights of stairs." They laughed, and then a comfortable silence lengthened.

"Are you back at Connor.com?"

"No. I'm not going back. I figure I can trust my future to God."

"That's great, Tess. Really great to hear."

She stalled, aware they'd been talking for over an hour, but she needed to tell him that she valued his integrity, his kindness. . . .

She bit her lip. "Hey, call me sometime."

"You, too. I'm home most days. If I'm not leave a message and—"

"You'll get back to me." She laughed.

When he spoke this time there was unevenness in his tone. "I think about you a lot."

"I think about you, too."

"What's the weather like in Chicago?" She needed him to keep talking so she could hear his voice.

"It sleeted today."

"Here, too." Dead air. "Well . . . talk to you soon."

She replaced the receiver and sat alone in the apartment.

The phone shrilled. She sat while the instrument cycled and the answering machine picked up. Len's agitated voice came over the line.

"What's with the box of nuts, Tess? And this note: 'Not interested.' Are these nuts supposed to represent your answer—some kind of a joke—is this your way of getting even? Have you lost your *mind?*"

Smiling, she rested her head on the back of the sofa. Maybe she had, Len. Right now it sure looked like it.

20

Tess came home from the post office Thursday afternoon to find a large manila envelope jammed in the mail receptacle. She had been waiting almost a month now for the right job opportunity to open up. She hoped this would be the answer to her prayers. Maneuvering the wrapper free, she caught her breath and held it when she saw that the letter was from Caltron—one of Denver's largest pharmaceutical companies.

Inside was the prize she sought. Was she available for a ten o'clock appointment on the eighteenth?

Was she ever.

The morning of the interview, she dressed carefully in a red wool suit and white silk blouse. She studied her image in the mirror, trying to decide if she should wear her hair up or down, changing earrings twice before she was satisfied that she looked appropriately professional.

Glancing at her watch, she picked up her purse and started out the door. Then she stopped. Her nerves were side-straddling her backbone.

Tossing her purse onto the couch, she dropped to her knees. She'd taken to praying more and more in the past month, until now, she couldn't imagine *not* taking her concerns to the Lord. She took a moment to collect her thoughts, desperately wanting to get this right.

"Dear Father in heaven." She paused. "Dear God, You have been so faithful to me, even when I wasn't aware of it. Help me to trust You, to know that no matter how this turns out, You're in control. I only need You—to know You more."

She relaxed once the words were said. A peace came over her.

"I desire to know and receive Your Spirit."

And she did—oh, how she did.

"I give You all my doubts and insecurities. I willingly place every facet of my life in Your hands, Father—I surrender all." Tears dripped from the corners of her eyes; she'd have to redo her makeup. "I respectfully remind You that there will be more times when I'll want to take it all back than times I will walk solely in faith, but I pray Your grace will not allow me to remain in the darkness for long.

"I need to know that You are walking beside

me—every day. I ask for the faith that Carter and Stella have—I want the peace and assurance as I leave this room today that my life is no longer temporal, but eternal, in Your service. . . ."

"Hey, McConnell."

"What's happenin', Nelson?" Carter fingered the cupid tie around his neck and grinned. Sure, the men at work razzed him for wearing the gift Tess had sent for Valentine's Day, but so what? It had her written all over it.

"I had a promising job interview today," she said.

Carter unwrapped a stick of spearmint gum and stuck it in his mouth. In the background, flight controllers went about their business. His eyes habitually focused on the blinking blips on radar.

"And?"

"I won't know for a few days."

"Well, I'll ask God to make a special dispensation in your case." His grin widened.

"How's the ol' stress level?" she asked.

"What stress?" He could sense her subsequent smile. "I've decided to look at my job differently—

I'm happy all those fly jockeys are fighting over me. I'm popular."

"Carter." She took a deep breath.

"Yo."

"I've accepted Jesus as my Savior. I did it awhile ago, but it's been sort of growing in me this past month. This morning though, it seemed very *real*."

His tone instantly sobered. "You did?"

"I'm taking baby steps," she confessed. "I'll need help from you."

"You don't become an adult overnight—you don't grow in Christ overnight. If you've placed the order, Tess, God will deliver. I'm so proud of you."

Shoot. Was that emotion suddenly crowding the back of his throat? Shoot. It was. He took a swipe at his eyes and chewed hard on his gum to control the surge of tears.

"I know you only have a few minutes for your break—I just wanted to tell you."

"Thanks." He spit the gum out in a tissue and leaned closer to the mouthpiece. "Hey. Nice work, Nelson."

"Thanks"—and here she drew not upon her *Dummies* guides, but upon her heart—"but the credit belongs to the Lord."

21

March arrived on the heels of strong winds, and kites began flapping in East Denver Park District. Tess's long-distance bills to Chicago were astronomical, but her new position with Caltron paid more than she had hoped.

When she'd gotten on that plane to Hawaii her life had been in shambles, and look what God had done.

Wonder flooded her anew. What a change a few weeks had brought. She wanted to tell Carter personally, to see him face to face. The idea brought her up short as she doodled on a scratch pad in her new office overlooking the Denver skyline.

Well, why not?

For less than one month's phone bill she could fly to Chicago and spend an entire weekend. She and Carter could talk without wondering about how the other person looked, without *wishing* that they could kiss each other good night.

Reaching for the phone, she gently eased the door shut with the tip of her leather shoe.

She drove to Denver International Airport on her lunch hour and sat in the car and studied the control tower, trying to envision Carter's world. Doubts assuaged her. Should she really fly to Chicago? Show up unannounced and uninvited? On the pretext of delivering a greeting card?

Feminists would have a cow.

Well, so what. She couldn't get through another week without seeing him. She sat with her window cracked so she could hear the roar of jets taking off and landing. Carter needed her. She *knew* he did. He needed someone to come home to. Someone to share his life, someone who would love him, care for him, nurture him—

He needed her and she needed him.

Together, with the Lord's blessing, they could conquer the world!

22

Tess Nelson handed the cabby a twenty and slid out of the backseat. She had an hour and a half to make the Chicago flight.

Sprinting toward the busy terminal, she ignored lingering ice patches still clinging to the walkways. Suddenly, she was slip-sliding across the frozen glaze, groping wildly for anything to latch onto for leverage.

Dropping her suitcase, she lunged for a handrail moments before she would have sprawled face first. But not quickly enough to prevent her left ankle from twisting.

Deja vu.

She grasped the injured appendage and groaned out loud. No! There was something about Denver International and ankles that didn't mix.

She took small comfort in the knowledge that her

right ankle had finally healed and this time it was her left that was rapidly ballooning. Picking up her suitcase, she limped on.

In a rush to board her flight, she limped right past the handsome man who had dashed out the exit door.

Carter skidded to a halt and whipped around when he saw Tess hobbling in the opposite direction, carrying luggage.

She was *leaving* town as he was arriving.

Panic seized him and he yelled, "Hey! What's wrong with your ankle now?"

Dropping his overnight bag, he sprinted after her, threading his way through a throng of oncoming passengers. "Nelson!"

The sound of Carter's voice brought Tess to a halt. "Carter?" She whirled, dropping her case when she spotted him, and raced toward him, oblivious to the pain.

Carter twirled her around as she latched onto his neck and held on tightly. Oh, he smelled *so* good! So Carter.

Catching her up in his arms, he kissed her, oblivious to the fact that they were blocking traffic flow.

"What are you doing here?" she exclaimed when they finally relinquished their hold.

"The oddest thing—I was trying to find a stamp to mail your St. Patrick's Day card, and I thought, 'Hey, McConnell, why don't you just take her the card in person?'"

She interrupted. "Carter! That was my line! And a lame one at that."

"No way."

"Way!" she argued.

He drew her back into his arms. "What are *you* doing here?"

"I'm going to see *you*."

"I'm *coming* to see you."

"Hey." His tone softened. "Aren't we blessed. We've both found what we're looking for." He leaned slightly to kiss the tip of her nose. The gesture promised a lifetime of commitment. "I love you, Tess Nelson."

Only through His grace could her life have taken such a wonderful turn, Tess realized. Only through God's grace.

"What made you change your mind—convince yourself that you can trust me and God?"

She smiled, tightening her hold around his neck. "If I can trust God, I can trust you."

He chuckled. "Lady, I hate to tell you, but you can trust God a lot more that you can trust me."

"Hey, McConnell, speaking of God," she grinned, then sobered, "thanks for the introduction."

He winked. "My pleasure."

Draping his arm around her waist, they walked back to the line of waiting taxis.

"Hey, Tess."

"Yes, Carter?"

"What would you think about me flying to Denver, say—for the next year, every weekend?"

He leaned to give her another kiss. Pausing, they stopped to hold each other as the crowd dodged around them. Finally, he stepped back and said softly, "Maybe you and I could go out to dinner those weekends—give ourselves a chance to get to know each other better?"

She nodded. "I'd say that is a definite go."

"Good." Carter suspected he already knew all he needed to know about Tess Nelson—but he wanted to enjoy their courtship. He picked up his flight bag and they continued toward the cabs, arm-in-arm. He glanced up at the lowering sky.

"Have you heard what the weather's going to do?"

"No," she said. "And I *don't* want to."

THE END

Dear Reader,

I wonder if you found *Stranded in Paradise* to be lighter reading than most Christian fiction? If you did, I'm glad! I truly believe laughter is sound medicine and a gift from God. In a world where we often experience sarcasm and bitterness, I'm so thankful God blessed us with the escape valve that enables us to smile in the midst of chaos and uncertainty!

So when I was asked to write a novel for the Women of Faith Fiction series, I happily resolved to make laughter a key ingredient in the novel. Since my husband and I visited Hawaii for the first time early this year, I knew that tropical location was another key ingredient for my novel. After all, the island is pure tropical paradise—the pineapple sweet and the vibrant rainbows a touch of heaven! But like everything else on earth, storms occasionally disturb the island's tranquility. And that understanding is the book's final and perhaps most profound ingredient.

My family has been richly blessed, but we still have personal storms that make us pause and examine our foundation. In such times of trouble, it helps me to realize that I'm not in charge of my day . . . God is. In his book *Day by Day*, Chuck Swindoll uses an illustration from the life of an oyster to aptly describe God's role in life's troubles. "An irritation occurs when the shell of the oyster is invaded by an alien substance—like a grain of sand. When that happens, all the resources within the tiny, sensitive oyster rush to the irritated spot and begin to release healing fluids that otherwise would have remained dormant. By and by the irritant is covered—by a pearl. Had there been no interruption, there could have been no pearl."

What a comforting thought to carry us through the God appointed storms of life! Through periods when we're forced to stop and ask, Is my spiritual foundation truly sound? Will the occasional upheavals sweep away my house, or hold firm to the solid rock? I like to think that my foundation is unwavering, but when the storms come, I all too often focus on the irritant. As the storm passes and bright sunshine suddenly breaks through a wall of clouds, God is there, where He's always been, guarding my foundation. Protecting His child, creating, if not a pearl, a stronger oyster.

Swindoll reminds the reader of J. B. Phillips's paraphrased James 1:2–4: "When all kinds of troubles and temptations crowd into your lives, my brothers, don't resent them as intruders, but welcome them as friends! Realize that they come to test your faith and to produce in you the quality of endurance . . . let the process go on until that endurance is fully developed, and you will find you have become men [and women] of mature character."

As you turn your thoughts to the reading group guide that follows, I hope you'll prayerfully reflect on the simple truths in *Stranded in Paradise*. How firm is your foundation? Is your spiritual house built on sand or solid rock?

And have you focused on the irritant or on the pearl?

I praise God for the opportunity to share my beliefs and my hope for eternity. May God richly bless each and every one of you.

Lori Copeland
Summer 2002

reading group guide

1. In the opening chapter of *Stranded in Paradise*, Tess Nelson loses her job—the job that she had given the bulk of her time and efforts to, to which she had devoted her very *life*. Discuss how this seemingly catastrophic incident initiates a bizarre series of events—a twisted ankle, lost luggage, a hotel fire, and a hurricane, to name a few—that remarkably lead to healing and restoration for Tess.

2. Carter McConnell's early encounters with Tess are less-than-perfect. As one of the first Christian characters Tess meets, how does Carter's "bad" behavior affect Tess's concept of Christians? Could his actions be considered beneficial—lending authenticity to his character?

3. Through flashbacks to Tess's childhood memories, we see that her early life was riddled with painful experiences. Discuss how this past pain shaped Tess's personality. Was her reaction to Carter's compassion and kindness emblematic of someone with her history?

4. At what point did it become obvious that Carter and Tess were drawn to each other by more than friendship? Did Carter, knowing that she was not a believer, handle himself with the appropriate amount of restraint? Did he, at any point, allow his emotions to control his actions? Discuss.

5. Stella DeMuer is an eccentric former movie star whose husband, Edgar, was wrongfully linked to the Communist Party in the McCarthy hearings. What influence did this elder woman's hospitality and personal story have on Tess's faith?

6. In the midst of Hurricane Alana, Tess does a great deal of soul-searching, considering the reality of God's love for her. What role did panic play in her eventual conversion? Do you believe panic is a common element used in evangelism? Is this good or bad?

7. Characteristic of her deliberate, thoughtful

nature, Tess decides she must return home to ponder all that has happened on her ill-fated vacation before submitting herself totally to God. Was this a wise decision? Why or why not?

8. Tess Nelson's tropical vacation in Maui was supposed to be *paradise*. Yet mishap after mishap seemed to indicate that this beautiful island was anything *but* celestial. Discuss the symbolism of Paradise—what it means in superficial, earthly terms and what it means in eternal, heavenly terms.

9. Upon her return to the states, Tess visits Mona, her mother. Removing her filter of anger, Tess sees Mona's life through new eyes. How does Tess's impression of her mother change? How do you think the relationship between these two women will evolve?

10. The character of Tess Nelson truly comes full-circle—quitting a job she previously devoted herself to, reaching out to a mother she once loathed, and embracing a God she never understood. Discuss the ramifications of Tess's past decisions and how God used even her disobedience to direct the path of her life.

acknowledgments

Thanks to E. W. Woolly, who showed the Copelands Maui for the first time, and then took time to read the manuscript and give me a "second opinion." Thanks, E.W. and Linda, for rainy luaus, sandy beaches, and extra sweet pineapple.

The following Internet Web sites provided important background information for this book:

Untied States Air Force Reserve

FEMA for Kids: Hurricanes

FEMA: Fact sheet: Hurricanes

Access NOAA: In The Eye of a Hurricane, Cmdr. Ron Philippborn, NOAA CORPS (retired)

USA Today; Weather Basics

Ask a Hurricane Hunter

Flight into a Hurricane

Astronomy and Earth Science: The Greatest Storm
on Earth

ABC News: Birth of a Hurricane

Stages of Development: The Growth of a Hurricane

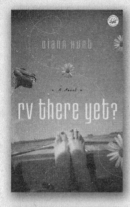

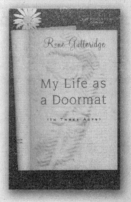

WOMEN OF FAITH™
fiction

COVENANT CHILD
A Story of Promises Kept

TERRI BLACKSTOCK

A Song I Knew by Heart

BRET LOTT
AUTHOR OF Jewel

a TIME *to* DANCE
A Story of Reconciliation

KAREN KINGSBURY

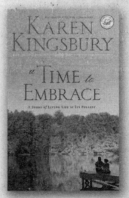

KAREN KINGSBURY

a TIME *to* EMBRACE
A Story of Living Life to Its Fullest

THOMAS NELSON
Since 1798

thomasnelson.com

WOMEN OF FAITH™
fiction

GARDENIAS FOR BREAKFAST

ROBIN JONES GUNN

stranded in paradise

SANDPEBBLES

PATRICIA HICKMAN